Rituraj stood at the entrance, a wide grin on his malicious face as he looked down at the fallen *Yuvaraja*. Stepping out of the door, he kicked Harischandra with a booted foot for good measure.

"Ritu, who's at the door?" Sitara walked into the living room whilst she was speaking to Rituraj.

"Why don't you come and see for yourself?" he invited her over.

Sitara had been under treatment for two and a half months and was feeling more confident, mentally and physically. One more month and they would be returning home. She walked to the entrance and her jaw dropped when she saw Harischandra in this pathetic condition. "Have you killed him?" she asked Rituraj in a stunned whisper.

He laughed softly. "How I wish! But no. The bastard's fainted. Do you want me to wake him up with a bucket of water, maybe?"

It was Sitara's turn to grin. "Allow me," she said, walking back into the flat to open the fridge. "But what is he doing here?"

Rituraj shrugged. "I didn't wait to find out."

ABOUT THE AUTHOR

Sundari Venkatraman is an Indie Author who has 62 books to her credit. These books have consistently featured in the Top 100 Bestseller Lists on Amazon Kindle, in both romance as well as Asian Drama categories. Her latest hot romances have all been on #1 Bestseller slot in Amazon India for over a month.

MAN FRIDAY is a standalone novel which is based on Indian Contemporary Royals. This kindle book remained in #1 Bestseller position on Amazon India for three months from its release.

Even as a child, Sundari absolutely loved the 'lived happily ever after' syndrome and she grew up on a steady diet of fairy tales, Phantom comics and Mandrake comics. It was always about good triumphing over evil and a happy ending after the protagonists surmounted all unexpected obstacles.

Once she entered her teens, Sundari switched her loyalties from fairy tales to Mills & Boon. While she loved reading both of these, she kept visualising what would have happened if there were similar situations happening in India; to local heroes and heroines. And of course, the joy of vanquishing the ubiquitous evil villains! Her imagination soared and she happily ensconced herself in a rosy romantic cocoon for many years.

Then came the writing—a true bolt from the blue! And Sundari Venkatraman has never looked back.

Books by Sundari Venkatraman

Standalone novels
The Malhotra Bride
Meghna
The Madras Affair
An Autograph for Anjali
Twin Torment
Finding Anya
Mr. Perfect
Man Friday
Her Prince Charming
Love in Agartha
Arjun's Penance
The Floundering Author
Ryan Finds a Bride
Tinder Loving Care
Shaan Gets Hitched
For Better or For Worse
Love… No Conditions Asked

Collection of shorts
Matches Made in Heaven
Tales of Sunshine

Marriages Made in India Series
#1 The Runaway Bridegroom
#2 Her Smitten Husband
#3 His Drunken Wife
#4 Her Secret Husband
#5 The Casanova's Wife
#6 Her Bohemian Husband

The Bansal Legacy Trilogy
#1 Simha International
#2 Rose Garden International
#3 Maharaja International

The Thakore Royals Trilogy
#1 The Marriage Predicament
#2 Tied in Knots
#3 The Wooing of the Shrew

The Groom Series Trilogy
#1 Groomnapped
#2 Gobsmacked
#3 Grounded

Written in the Stars Series
#1 Scorpio Superstar
#2 Leo's Desire
#3 Taurus Temptation
#4 Virgo's Krush
#5 Libra's Flame

Arora Iyers Trilogy
#1 Once Bitten Twice Lucky
#2 Heartthrob
#3 Call of the Heart

Dashavatar (Indian Mythology)
MATSYA: The First Avatar
KURMA: The Second Avatar
VARAHA: The Third Avatar
NARASIMHA: The Fourth Avatar
VAMANA: The Fifth Avatar
PARASHURAMA: The Sixth Avatar

The Princess Series (Historical Romance)
#1 The Passionate Princess
#2 The Rebel Princess

The Writer's Toolkit (Non-fiction)
Publishing Your Book on Amazon KDP

Bollywood Bros Trilogy
#1 Sing For Me
#2 Dance With Me

Romantic Shorts Series
#1 Chahti Hoon Tumhe
#2 Beauty is but Skin Deep
#3 Madeinheaven.com
#4 An Arranged Match
#5 The Reluctant Bride
#6 Shweta ka Swayamvar
#7 Pappa's Girl
#8 Red Rose Dating Agency
#9 Rahat Mili
#10 Reema's Matchmakers
#11 The Matchmaker's Dream

Man Friday

A romance novel by

SUNDARI VENKATRAMAN

FLAMING SUN

Cover Illustration: Unaiza Merchant
Editor: Preeti Arora
Marketed by: The Book Club

Baroda, 2018

"Please sit down, Sitara," said Rituraj, his voice firm. He wasn't sure how the Princess of Baroda would handle the news he was about to impart.

"What happened, Rituraj?" Sitara Devi asked her personal assistant, a gentle query evident in the way she raised her shapely eyebrow. She did follow his advice though and plonked herself rather abruptly on the low-slung sofa.

"Er… Prince Rajvardhan called. Just a few minutes ago." Rituraj backtracked and asked, "Would you like to speak with him? Let me call him back. I'm sure he would rather tell you personally. Though actually he asked me to…" Rituraj was prevaricating, wishing he didn't have to break this unexpected news to her.

Sitara studied his handsome face, trying to fathom what he was not telling her. It wasn't like Rituraj Srivastava to run away from situations. "We'll call him as soon as you tell me what has happened. You know, right?" There was a glimmer of amusement in her deep grey eyes as she watched him stuttering and wriggling. Well, it definitely was a sight to behold—six feet, two inches of steel and muscle actually squirming.

Unable to refuse her, he said, "Raja Harischandra Gajanan is no more. He…"

"What?" Sitara jumped up from the sofa as if released from a catapult. For a split second she stared at Rituraj in a daze. Colour ran high on her cheeks before receding, leaving her face a pale oval. It was only a few days ago that she had finally spoken about the disgrace and abuse she had suffered at her ex-husband Harischandra Gajanan's hands. That too, she had given verbal evidence to a magistrate. She had done it at Prince Rajvardhan Thakore's request since Gajanan was insisting on marrying the prince's girlfriend. Gajanan genuinely believed he needed a third wife. It was incredible to hear that the man was actually dead.

Rituraj walked up to her and took her slender hand in his, shaking his head slowly from side to side. "I've never been more serious in my entire life. He accidentally killed himself in his own palace. A heavy brass chandelier fell on him, crushing him to death."

"When? And how did that happen?" Sitara's heart was beating erratically, multiple thoughts scrambling through her mind as she swiftly recalled her life with the man—no, demon—she had been married to almost a couple of decades ago.

Rituraj wasn't aware that he was gently stroking her trembling hand as he replied, "Barely an hour ago. The police had gone to his palace with an arrest warrant. Prince Rajvardhan Thakore and Princess Chitrangada Vasudeva were present in the Gajanan Palace. Raja Harischandra Gajanan lost his temper and fired his gun randomly towards the ceiling. I believe three bullets hit the chandelier and it fell on him. He died on the spot." His voice was soothing as he spoke to the princess and it was with great difficulty that he managed not to throw his arms around her and hug her close. After all, she had been married to the man for almost two years, even if there had been no love lost between them. Would she get affected by his sudden death?

Sitara digested the information slowly even as a small smile broke out on her face. She looked up at Rituraj and grinned. "You mean Harry is really dead."

Rituraj's gentle brown gaze shone with mischief as he gazed at her radiant face, glad to see she wasn't upset. "Yes, that's exactly what has happened." A faint smile appeared on his gentle face.

Princess Sitara Devi threw back her head and laughed uproariously. "And may his soul rot in hell!"

"Amen!" Rituraj added his fervent wish to hers.

Baroda, 2001

Rituraj stood next to one of the elaborately carved marble pillars that held up the domed ceiling of the palace, not knowing what had hit him as he stared at Princess Sitara Devi when she got out of the car. She appeared broken, not just physically, but as if her soul had wilted. As if… as if she could never become whole again. Never one to be fat, the tall princess seemed to have lost a lot of weight, making her appear emaciated.

He stared in shock at her once beautiful face which used to remind him of the moon on *Purnima* nights. What happened to make it so dull and colourless? As if it was sepia-tinted? He shook his head, dazed. Rani Vasundhara Devi Gaekwad of Baroda, Sitara's mother, had told him with tears pouring down her face, that the princess was on her way home as her husband didn't want her any more. Prince Harischandra Gajanan was going to file for a divorce.

To be truthful, that particular information had hit Rituraj directly like an arrow to his heart. He still wasn't sure whether it made him feel sorry for her or happy for himself. Yes, Rituraj had realised he was in love with Princess Sitara Devi Gaekwad exactly when

Raja Harischandra Gajanan was placing the *sindoor* in her *maang*, which was one of the most important rituals of a traditional Hindu wedding. That had been less than two years ago. Rituraj had felt a terrible pain in his heart, when it had struck him that Sitara could never be his.

He had tried his best not to fall in love with her. Whenever thoughts about Sitara entered his mind he immediately immersed himself in work. He was the only child of the accountant-cum-manager of the kingdom. Aspiring to marry the princess could only create grief for all people concerned! Even though India had become a republic in 1950, the royals still maintained protocol. A common man like himself, even if he lived in the palace, couldn't aspire to marry the princess.

But then, when has the path of true love ever followed a logical route? Not with Romeo-Juliet, nor with Heer-Ranjha. But at least in those love stories, the passion was mutual. In his case, Rituraj knew that it was a one-sided love which was doomed to fail. Rituraj allowed the love of his life to slip out of his hands and even his close friends had no idea about the extent of his feelings.

His anxious gaze followed the princess as she walked into the palace along with her father, Raja Manvendra Singh Gaekwad, her steps hesitant, as if she had grown old and feeble in the twenty-two months since her marriage. She had never visited her parents' home after the wedding. Rituraj fisted his hands and dug in his feet. It was an effort to stop himself from rushing over to her and gathering her in his arms. She appeared so unloved, the young princess of eighteen-going-on-nineteen who used to be her parents' cherished child. His dark eyes shimmered with unshed tears as he felt her agony deep within him as if it was his own.

"Sitara..." he called out in an anguished whisper, unable to restrain himself.

She turned to look at Rituraj with no expression in her deep grey eyes. She could have been dead for the lack of reaction—except that she continued to breathe and walk—before her gaze returned to the floor as she continued to walk in the direction of the wide, marble staircase.

Rani Vasundhara Devi Gaekwad came rushing down the stairs to meet her daughter halfway down the hall, forgetting for once to act like the graceful queen she was. "Sitara, my *bachcha!*" Vasundhara Devi gathered her daughter in her arms, tears pouring down her wrinkled face.

Rituraj's eyes went wide with horror as he noticed the lack of reaction in Sitara. The princess stopped in her tracks when her mother threw her arms around her, but didn't bother to greet the older woman or hug her back. It was as if she was bound by some kind of dark power which simply refused to release its hold on her.

"May I go to my room?" Sitara asked her mother in a hoarse whisper, her gaze fixed on the wall behind her mother's shoulder, as if the painting of her ancestor riding on a horse had caught her complete attention.

Manvendra Singh gave a small shake of his head when his wife turned her concerned gaze upon him. "Why don't you ask Nirupama to serve tea? I'm sure Sitara would love to have a cup. I know I'm dying for one."

Rituraj immediately moved forward. "Let me order for tea, Rani *ma*," he said, before walking to the kitchen located towards the rear of the palace.

Sitara went to the sofa when her father took her hand and guided her to it, her mother following them, a hand on her daughter's painfully thin arm.

Vasundhara Devi wrapped her left arm around her daughter's bony shoulders, holding her close against her own warmth.

Sitara lay her head on her mother's shoulder, like a child, shutting her eyes even as she took a deep, shuddering breath. She still couldn't believe the nightmare was over, the one where she had been the evil Harischandra Gajanan's wife. Was it really possible that she had escaped the devil and still emerged alive? It all seemed so incredible to her.

Rituraj walked back into the hall, a servant following him, carrying a silver tea service on a matching, ornate tray. He began pouring the fragrant tea into three cups, adding milk and sugar, exactly how each of the royal trio was accustomed to drinking it. Placing tiny silver spoons on the saucers, he handed the teacups to the Raja first, then the Rani, before eyeing Sitara. Did she still have the strength to hold the cup in her hands? He stared at her hands as they lay on her lap, the blue veins standing out against her translucent white skin. He had read the phrase, 'skin and bone' a number of times in books. He was seeing it for the first time, as he stared completely aghast at the princess's thin hands. Had they fed her at all?

"Sitara…" Vasundhara spoke softly to her daughter, "will you have some tea, darling?"

Sitara opened her eyes in a half slit before lifting her head from her mother's shoulder. "I wouldn't mind some." She took the teacup from Rituraj's hand, her gaze vacant when she looked into his eyes. "Thank you," she said, uttering the words automatically, like a well-oiled machine. She drank the tea without tasting it before repeating her earlier words, "May I go to my room?"

Vasundhara Devi turned to her husband, a helpless expression on her face which didn't sit well as the Rani of Baroda was always firm and decisive.

Manvendra Singh gave his wife a small, reassuring nod, taking his daughter's hand in his. "Come, my dear, let me take you up to your room."

Sitara got up immediately and went along with her father, unaware of the worried pairs of eyes following her.

"What has he done to my daughter, Rituraj?" Vasundhara Devi moaned, shutting her eyes and burying her head in her hands.

"Rani *ma*!" Though Rituraj's voice was soft, it was firm as he took Vasundhara Devi's hands in his. "You have to remain strong, Rani *ma*. Sitara Devi needs your strength, more than ever."

Tears shimmered in Vasundhara Devi's eyes as she looked up at the strapping young man who had been like a son to her since he moved into their palace a decade ago. Her hands clinging to his manly ones, she said in a broken voice, "I have never seen my Sitara like this. She has always been a cheerful and happy child, truly lighting up our lives. I can't believe what must have happened to her that she seems so... so impassive, as if she has lost interest in life."

Rituraj couldn't help but agree with Vasundhara Devi. Without a thought to her royal status, he threw an arm around her and gave her a tight hug, talking like a wise old man when he said, "It was you who told me that time is a great healer, Rani *ma*. And isn't that the truth? The princess will recover, please don't worry. It's a good thing she's back home here at the Gaekwad Palace." He was but speaking from experience. Losing his parents in an accident was a memory stored deep within his mind, which had faded very gradually over the last decade.

Vasundhara Devi buried her face in Rituraj's shoulder and wept unashamedly.

3

Vinayak Garodia stared in awe at the young man pounding away at the punching bag. Rituraj Srivastava had come to him to learn boxing barely two years ago, and was as good as a pro in a really short span of time. It was also because he had been diligent in working out for a minimum of five days in a week. And he kept away for two days only because Vinayak refused to let him practise without a break.

Right now, it was obvious Rituraj was taking out his frustrations on the practicing equipment and his master was only glad that it wasn't an opponent's face. *What must have upset the boy?* Vinayak couldn't help wondering.

Having known the Gaekwad royal family since many years, Vinayak had also known Rituraj from the time he was a baby. When the seventeen-year-old had joined his boxing classes, he had realised almost immediately that something was eating at Rituraj's insides. He had befriended him over the next few weeks and had soon become his confidante, privy to his frustrated love for the Gaekwad princess.

When Rituraj paused to wipe the sweat off his upper body, Vinayak asked, "What happened to set you off now?" his voice gentle.

Rituraj turned to glare at the older man, forgetting for a moment that Vinayak was his master, whom he always treated with great respect. "Why do you ask?" he growled, before adding, "*Masterji*," as a complete afterthought. Not just the words but even his tone remained brusque to the point of being curt.

Vinayak grinned, walking towards the other man and placing a hand on his shoulder. "Well, all I can say is I know you almost as well as you know yourself. Come on, out with it. What's up?"

Rituraj blew out his breath in a deep, 'Phew!' before making an effort to calm down. "Princess Sitara Devi is back home for good."

Vinayak raised an enquiring eyebrow. "For good means exactly what?"

"Her husband, that bastard Harischandra Gajanan, is divorcing her." Rituraj didn't feel it was wrong to share the information with his boxing instructor since the royal family wasn't keeping it a secret from anyone. And Vinayak Garodia wasn't one to gossip anyway.

"Hmm. Is the princess terribly unhappy about it?" Vinayak felt sad for the young princess. To begin with, he couldn't really understand why they had got Princess Sitara Devi married at the tender age of sixteen. Now, she was going to get a divorce when she was barely eighteen. How sad was that!

"Yes!" Rituraj bunched his fists, his body automatically going into fighter mode when he thought of her. "She's horrendously unhappy," he said, gnashing his teeth. *What wouldn't I give to have Yuvaraja Harischandra Gajanan in the ring for just two minutes! How dare he treat a gentle soul like Sitara in such a callous fashion?*

"Did you find out what's she's upset about?"

Rituraj frowned fiercely at his instructor, his thick and dark eyebrows meeting above his fiery brown eyes. "I don't understand. It must be because that heartless brute has thrown her out of his life, right?"

Vinayak Garodia shook his head slowly from side to side. "Listen, Rituraj. I have heard some tales about Harischandra Gajanan, none of them pleasant. For all you know, the princess had a lucky escape if he decided to let go of her. She is young enough to re-build her own life."

There was a look of surprise on Rituraj's face as he stared at Vinayak. "What are you saying, *Masterji*? What have you heard?"

Vinayak wasn't sure how much to let on to Rituraj. After all, Rituraj was also just about nineteen and not all that worldly wise. He had had a protective upbringing at the palace under the aegis of the Raja and Rani of Gaekwad. He couldn't very well tell the boy that *Yuvaraja* Gajanan was a sexual pervert. But the Gajanan prince was also infamous for his violent nature. He took pleasure in hurting all those weaker than him and most especially women. Vinayak said in an expressionless voice, "I've heard that the *Yuvaraja* of Indore is a cruel man. He has no qualms about beating up the palace servants and his horses. He enjoys inflicting pain on those around him. Gives him a huge high."

Rituraj turned pale on hearing Vinayak's words. Would her husband really have beaten the gentle Sitara Devi? But she had been a little more than a child when she married the man. And he was almost double her age. How could he be so cruel? Rituraj's heart bled for the princess. "Are you sure you have your information correct, *Masterji*? He's a royal himself, dammit. How could he behave in such an uncouth manner? Shouldn't he be protecting his subjects instead of hurting them himself?" Rituraj demanded to know.

Vinayak would have laughed if he hadn't been sure it would irritate Rituraj all the more. And it wasn't a funny matter whichever way you looked at it. It was about how ignorant and innocent Rituraj was. It was obvious that Harischandra Gajanan was one of those royals who believed that he could get away with evil deeds all because he was a prince. Vinayak shrugged, saying, "Well, he probably thinks that he has greater license all because he is a royal."

Rituraj did an about turn and went back to punching the bag or he might have smashed something, such was his temper.

Vinayak sighed, shaking his head to himself. Maybe he should be happy that his other students were fairly attuned to Rituraj in his violent mood and kept away from the training ring after noticing the treatment the punching bag was receiving on that particular day.

Poor Rituraj! The instructor now felt sorrier for his student than for the Gaekwad princess. After all, he had seen the way the young man had slogged at picking up the pieces of his young life which had fallen apart after the love of his life got married to another man and went away!

He couldn't suppress the rising spark of hope he felt on his protégé's behalf. Maybe one day the princess would notice how Rituraj loved her from the bottom of his heart.

Baroda, 1992

A ten-year-old Rituraj looked at Raja Manvendra Singh Gaekwad with tears rolling down his chubby cheeks. Both his parents had died in a train accident two days ago and being an only child, he was all alone in the world. What was going to happen to him?

Before the Raja could say anything, Rani Vasundhara Devi walked forward to hug the little boy, running a gentle hand over his dark head, calmly waiting for the tears to subside. "Don't think you have no parents, my child. We will always be there for you. You must come to live here in the palace with us."

He had been living in an outhouse in the palace grounds ever since he could remember. In fact, his mother had mentioned a number of times that she had given birth to him right there in that very outhouse.

Rituraj moved his head away to look up at the Rani's face as if to see if she was serious. Seeing the affection in her dark eyes, Rituraj bravely wiped his tears away and gave her a small smile, nodding his head.

Vasundhara Devi took his hand in hers and walked with him up the marble staircase which lay in the centre of the main hall, turning left when they reached the first floor. Walking down the corridor, she stopped at the third room on the right. Opening the door, she said, "This will be your room from now on."

Rituraj's dark eyes glowed as he stared at the grand room. While his house was by no means small, this was something else altogether. There was a huge four-poster bed in the middle of the room that seemed to be out of this world. He turned to look up at Vasundhara Devi and said, "Thank you, Rani *ma*."

"You are welcome, Rituraj. You know that Harshvardhan's room is next to yours and Sitara's is before that, right?" Prince Harshvardhan Singh Gaekwad was her three-year-old son and Princess Sitara Devi Gaekwad was her older daughter who was all of nine years old.

Rituraj nodded his head vigorously. He had always had the run of the palace and knew everything there was to know, even the hidden passages and the secret tunnel, though he had never succeeded in exploring them. His father had forbidden him from walking beyond the large stone door that passed off for a wall, hiding the tunnel behind it. It was said that the tunnel connected to a chamber beneath the cultural museum which was at least fifteen kilometres away from the palace.

"You will have your meals with us and continue your education in the school you love." The Rani was hoping the boy would cheer up a little. "I will ask *Munshiji* to speak to your school principal and do the needful." She didn't elaborate that she and the Raja would now become his official guardians.

A servant knocked on the door before walking in with two large trunks. Brijmohan had packed Rituraj's clothes, books and family photographs and brought them over to the room allotted for him.

The two of them—Brijmohan and Rituraj—unpacked everything and placed all his stuff in the ornately carved wardrobes made of teakwood. Vasundhara Devi and Brijmohan pretended not to notice when Rituraj wiped his eyes with his small hands as he placed the framed photographs of his parents right at the front of the wardrobe.

"I'll sleep in one corner of this room. You don't need to worry about being alone." Brijmohan whispered to the little boy, as if it was their secret. He was actually doing it at the Rani's suggestion.

Rituraj threw both his arms around the older man's waist and hugged him tightly, burying his face in his chest.

Brijmohan hugged the child back, unable to stop the tears flowing from his eyes. After all, it was Rituraj's father who had trained Brijmohan in his duties at the palace.

The pain of losing his parents reduced over the next few weeks, what with the excitement of living in the palace and getting to be friends with Princess Sitara Devi. Rituraj even got to play big brother to young Prince Harshvardhan Singh.

Baroda, 1999

The years rolled by and it was time for Princess Sitara Devi to wed. The whole palace took on a festive air as the wedding of the sixteen-year-old princess to the twenty-eight-year-old *Yuvaraja* Harischandra Gajanan of Indore was celebrated at the Baroda palace over four days with pomp and ceremony.

At seventeen, Rituraj did a lot of work at the wedding. In fact, he didn't give himself time to think. After all, the thought of Princess Sitara Devi getting married to a stranger and leaving the palace created a strange disturbance within him. His throat felt choked with emotions which he was simply unable to define.

Sitara and Rituraj had grown up together in the palace, with Harshvardhan tagging along most of the time. It had been fun, going on long horse rides in the mornings and then going to school together. Rituraj liked to chat with Sitara who was intelligent and a wonderful conversationalist. They did argue at times, but their core relationship always stayed unaffected.

It had never occurred to Rituraj before the wedding ceremony that maybe he was harbouring some tender feelings towards the Gaekwad princess.

First and foremost, it was gratitude which Rituraj felt towards the Raja and Rani of Baroda. While he adored the prince and princess, he wasn't sure at which point his feelings towards the princess had changed from gratitude to something else altogether, something beyond friendliness.

Even now, he wasn't able to articulate his emotions towards Sitara. If someone had told him that he had fallen in love with her and wanted her for himself, he would have been truly dismayed. After all, how could he think of the princess as his equal? Her parents were affectionate and kind towards him and over time he had become a part of the close-knit family. But Rituraj would never allow himself to forget that he was merely the son of their once-upon-a-time manager and accountant.

Rituraj felt as if his heart was being squeezed hard, his eyes tearing up when he watched Raja Harischandra Gajanan place the *mangalsutra* around Princess Sitara Devi's neck and fill *sindoor* in her *maang*—the rites making sure she belonged to the *Yuvaraja* of Indore now.

This was it! Sitara was leaving him—Rituraj, her best friend—and going to live in a stranger's home, as his wife. Why? Why couldn't she have stayed here at the Gaekwad Palace for some more years? What was the hurry to be married anyway? She was barely sixteen.

It had never struck Rituraj before now, not the whole of last week when the other ceremonies were taking place. He had been happy enough, helping with all the tasks while supervising the palace servants. He had even teased Sitara about the *mehendi* she was wearing.

"That's so yuck!" Rituraj told her, eyeing Sitara's hands and legs decked with *mehendi*.

She pouted at him. "How typical of a man! We women like it."

"Are you sure? Or do you feel forced to like it? It does smell strange, you know." He scrunched up his nose, indicating that he didn't care for the smell.

Sitara got up and in a flash, drew her forefinger down his cheek, laughing when he yelled at the streak of *mehendi* across his face.

But, Rituraj swallowed hard, his Adam's apple bobbing, even then he hadn't realised she was another man's wife first. Sitara and Rituraj's friendship would survive only if *Yuvaraja* Harischandra Gajanan did not disapprove.

Now, *Yuvaraja* Harischandra Gajanan had tied the knot with Sitara and she wholly belonged to him.

Unable to bear the pain anymore, and not able to bring back the smile that had gone missing from his cheerless face, Rituraj stepped out of the hall and into the garden, completely shaken.

Would she miss him? He didn't know about that. But what he knew for sure by now was that it felt as if his heart was being pulled out of his chest and squeezed mercilessly. The pain was unbearable, much more than what he had felt at the time when his parents had died unexpectedly.

He went to sit on a wrought iron chair which was placed at the far end of the gazebo where climbers trailed. He was confident that no one would find him there, at least not all that easily.

Princess Sitara Devi's eyes searched in vain for Rituraj, as they checked every nook and cranny of the marble hall located in the Gaekwad Palace where her wedding ceremony had taken place barely a couple of hours ago. He was nowhere to be found.

Sitara realised that she couldn't very well walk away from her new husband, even if he let go of her hand that he held firmly in his. She didn't want to leave before saying 'bye' to her best and closest friend. Her *sasural* was in Indore and she wouldn't be visiting often.

Where was Rituraj? Hadn't he been standing next to his favourite pillar not far from the entrance to the hall? There were a number of times when Sitara had teased him about being an extension of that pillar, the first of a dozen of those, which decorated the palace hall. It was from there that he watched the happenings in the palace, supervising the footmen and ensuring the comfort of the royal family.

"I need the washroom." She turned and spoke to her new husband, her gaze fixed on his chin.

"As long as you promise to return to me immediately." Harischandra Gajanan laughed loudly, enjoying the colour rushing up his bride's cheeks. She was shy, Princess Sitara Devi, like a young filly needing to be broken. Oh, he definitely was looking forward to the *suhaag raat*.

"I will," said Sitara, relieved when he let go of her hand. She swiftly walked to the rear of the palace, refusing to look to the right or to the left in case someone stopped to speak with her. She stepped out of the rear entrance and into the garden, looking for Rituraj.

"Ritu," she called softly to begin with before raising her voice as she walked further and further away from the palace. It was a good thing everyone was busy with the wedding lunch. She soon began to run in the direction of the gazebo since she knew it was one of his favourite places. She wasn't really surprised when she found Rituraj sitting there. He was slumped on the bench and his posture conveyed a feeling of gloom and despair. "What are you doing here?" she asked, staring at the back of his head.

Rituraj got up immediately, rubbing a hand over his eyes before turning and giving Sitara a shocked look. "What are *you* doing here?" he asked. "You must return to the palace immediately, Princess Sitara Devi, before they send a search party."

Sitara laughed softly. "Even a newly married princess needs the bathroom sometimes, right? My husband will ensure no one comes looking for me. But tell me something, why are you hiding here, Ritu? I thought you were the one in charge of my wedding ceremony. And when were you going to return to the palace?" She gave him a reproachful look, before continuing, "Don't you have plans to join the family for lunch? And you know what? I'll be leaving the palace soon after we finish our meal."

Her words dug into him, deeply. Rituraj clenched his hands into fists, gritting his teeth to bring about some semblance of control. He wanted to tear at his hair and beat his chest, and scream at the universe for cheating him of what he thought was rightfully his. Why? Why did Sitara have to belong to someone else? *Yuvaraja* Harischandra Gajanan would be taking her far away from Rituraj, the person who loved her more than he loved himself.

"Hey, what happened to you? Aren't you talking to me anymore?" Sitara's friendly smile had disappeared by now as she looked at her friend. Rituraj appeared tense about something. What could have happened? "Is something wrong, Ritu?" she asked, laying a hand on her arm.

Rituraj jumped back as if burned, shaking his head. "No, Princess Sitara. There's nothing really wrong. It's just that I happen to have a headache. You please go and join your husband. I'll see you soon."

Sitara laughed. "You have a headache? You, who never falls sick? I refuse to believe it. And what's with the Princess bit, huh? I am Sitara, your best and closest buddy. Or have you forgotten?"

Rituraj looked at her innocent face and wanted to scream in agony. Had he been stupid, maybe? Would the Raja and Rani have accepted him as their son-in-law since they already treated him like their son? But then, until the wedding took place, he hadn't even known he was in love with Sitara. *No, I am not just stupid, but an absolute idiot.* He took a deep breath, doing his best to calm down, but still refused to meet Sitara's grey gaze that had turned steely. "But then, you are married to the *Yuvaraja* of Indore. It won't be right if I address you by your first name," he said softly, looking down at his feet.

Sitara folded her arms against her chest, leaning on the wall as she looked him up and down. Rituraj was definitely acting strange. Only she wasn't able to put her finger on what was bothering him. Headache! Uff! What nonsense! He was as strong as a horse and had never, ever fallen sick in all the time she had known him, which was forever. He had come to live in the palace after his parents' deaths, but even before that, he had been living in the same compound as the palace, just a couple of hundred metres away.

"Okay, Mr. Srivastava, have it your way." She turned around to walk back to the palace. For one thing, her husband was waiting for her. And for another, she was confident that Rituraj would follow her. Hadn't he always done that?

Rituraj looked at Sitara who was walking away from him, tears blurring his eyesight, his body hunched in defeat. No, he simply would not be able to see *Yuvaraja* Harischandra Gajanan holding her hand and whispering into her ear. He turned to look the other way; his stance stiff as he worked hard at gaining control of his rampaging emotions. At seventeen, he hadn't mastered the art of hiding his feelings. Which was exactly the reason why he didn't want to be around when Sitara left with her husband to begin a new life in Indore.

Sitara was astonished when she turned around to check if Rituraj was following her and found him standing right where she had left him. And even worse, he had turned his face away from her and stayed that way, resolutely staring in the opposite direction. The surprise slowly turned into shock when she realised that he just wasn't going to spend time with her, the little bit that they had before she left. Then her shock transformed into anger as she ran away from the spot. So, let him not come. *As if I care*!

Indore, 2001

"Why don't you mind your own business, Father?" Harischandra Gajanan's voice was as steely as his piercing grey gaze when he glared at Digvijay Gajanan, the Raja of Indore. At thirty, the *Yuvaraja* felt he was way too old to listen to his aged parent.

Digvijay glared at his only offspring, disgust and temper warring for supremacy in his gaze as he shook his head at the younger man. *Where did I go wrong?* Harischandra had been nothing but trouble even when he was a toddler. Traces of violence were obvious in the way he broke his toys while playing with them; and later the limbs of his horses while learning to ride. But neither parent, Digvijay nor Jhalkaribai Gajanan, had taken the incidents seriously, too enamoured by their only male child, their *waaris*.

The worst of Harischandra's qualities had come to the fore, or rather, to his parents' notice, when he began to torture his young wife. At sixteen, Princess Sitara Devi had been twelve years younger than her husband at the time of their marriage.

Foolishly, both the Raja and Rani of Indore had believed that their son would mellow down once he had a loving spouse to take care of. Keeping this fact in mind they had chosen the gentle and beautiful Sitara as their daughter-in-law. Destiny of course chose a different route. Simply put, nothing had gone according to their plans. In the first few weeks of marriage, the royal duo didn't pay much attention to what was happening in the newly married couple's lives.

Sitara came down to breakfast one morning, her left cheek swollen and red. No amount of makeup could manage to hide it. "Is something wrong, *beti*?" asked Jhalkaribai, highly disturbed at the sight.

Sitara refused to look the older woman in the eye as she gave a small shake of her head, "No, Mother."

Jhalkaribai walked closer to her daughter-in-law and touched her cheek with an index finger and was shocked to find it hot. She placed the back of her hand against Sitara's forehead and realised that the younger woman was running a temperature. "You have fever, Sitara. You should be in bed."

Sitara raised her tortured gaze to meet her mother-in-law's eyes for a moment before looking down at her feet once again. Bed! No! She was terrified of her bed. That was where her husband did things to her that she never wanted to think about, let alone talk of. "I am alright, Mother. I…"

"Listen to me, Sitara." Jhalkaribai's voice was commanding as she pressed Sitara's shoulder to make her sit down. Turning around, the Rani called out to a servant to bring some tea immediately. She made Sitara drink two cups of the hot brew before she gently commanded her to have some breakfast.

Sitara chewed her way through one whole *mattar ki kachori* which was actually her favourite breakfast snack. Only it tasted like sawdust. She almost choked on the last bite when she heard footsteps, the firm tread suggesting it was her husband.

Sitara shut her eyes and took deep breaths, doing her best to calm her wildly beating heart. The fear, however, simply refused to go away. Her husband, Harischandra Gajanan, was a cruel and sadistic man. He got a kick out of beating and torturing anyone who crossed his path. It was unfortunate that Sitara bore the major brunt of his sadistic behaviour since she became his wife.

She wondered how her parents would react to the information if they got to know, even as she mentally shook her head. They would never get to know about it. It was such a shameful situation that Sitara didn't have the guts to talk to any living soul about the humiliation she suffered at Harischandra's hands day after day.

"Good morning, Mother." Harischandra greeted Jhalkaribai even as he sat down in the chair next to his wife, not missing the tremors running through her slender body. Pretending not to notice anything untoward, he continued to speak to the Rani, "Where's Father gone? Has he already had his breakfast?"

Jhalkaribai looked at her son with a trace of anger in her gaze. "Your father had an early morning meeting. He will return only in time for lunch. But listen Harry, Sitara…"

Harischandra lifted a hand to stop his mother from continuing the conversation. "…is my wife and hence she's my business. I don't want to hear anything you might want to say about her." He turned to his silent wife and said mockingly, "Am I not right, my darling Sitara? I'll never allow my mother to boss over you, my dear. You can rest assured on that count." He laughed as if he had cracked a joke and yelled for a servant. "Get me some scrambled eggs and toast. I don't want to eat this oily *kachori*, do you hear? And soon." The hint of violence was always present in *Yuvaraja* Harischandra Gajanan's voice, especially when he spoke to the servants.

"But Harry, you very well know I am anything but a troublesome mother-in-law." Jhalkaribai clenched her hands into fists as she spoke firmly to her son. "Sitara is running a temperature. She needs a doctor and some rest, in that order."

Harischandra sighed dramatically. "Why the hell can't I have some peace in my own home? Will you keep quiet for a while, Mother? At least until I finish my breakfast and get out of this bloody palace? Or would you rather I left without eating?" His voice was silky while his gaze was threatening as he looked at Jhalkaribai.

The Rani kept her silence, well aware that her son was capable of smashing everything in sight and wouldn't care who got hurt in the process. And she understood Sitara needed a respite from Harischandra, more than anyone else. She held Sitara's hand in hers, hoping to pacify the younger woman who had been so unfortunate as to tie the knot with her son.

That day was simply the beginning of the parents' suffering. Harischandra continued to ill-treat his wife, more openly now, while his parents were silent witnesses to his atrocities. The loving elderly couple ignored the black eyes and bruises. While Digvijay Singh and Jhalkaribai were completely ignorant about the degradation Sitara Devi suffered at her husband's hands in bed. When they had guests over often Sitara Devi did not come out of her room as her face was many a time badly disfigured. A few months later, Digvijay Gaekwad made up his mind and summoned the courage to speak with his son.

Digvijay Gaekwad was horrified to know that Harischandra had decided to divorce his wife and send her home to her parents. He immediately rebuked Harischandra angrily, saying, "It is my business when you send the daughter-in-law of our family back to her parents after being married to her for less than two years." He snarled at his son, his steely gaze piercing the younger man's. "I am answerable to the Raja and Rani of Gaekwad since I have taken responsibility for their daughter when I arranged the marriage between our royal families."

Harischandra felt a strong urge to throttle the old man. Why did he have to support someone else, every time? Why not favour his own child for a change? That is how it had always been. The Raja found fault with whatever Harischandra did. The *Yuvaraja* completely overlooked the fact that the Raja felt responsible for all the harm his son meted out to people he believed who could be easily bullied. And since he was royalty, that included pretty much everybody he interacted with. It upset Digvijay there was no way he could make his son see sense.

"You should have checked if the said daughter-in-law was fertile enough to bear a child, my heir, before arranging the wedding, Father," Harischandra roared at his parent.

"What? What are you saying?"

"You heard me the first time. But let me repeat, just in case. Your dear daughter-in-law is sterile. She's not fit to deliver the next generation of the royal Gajanans. Are you clear now?"

"Are you sure about that? How do you know?" It was Jhalkaribai's anxious voice questioning him now.

Harischandra lifted a large mirror in a carved wooden frame from where it hung on the wall and threw it down on the marble floor, watching with satisfaction when it smashed to smithereens even as the wooden frame broke into three, the debris scattered all over the Rani's sitting room. He turned to look at his parents and was excited to see the shock on their faces. Good! That should teach them a lesson. Next time nobody would dare to question his actions.

"How does a man get to know his wife is sterile? By performing medical tests, of course." Harischandra had no qualms as he lied through his teeth. "I, unlike the foolish Raja and Rani of Indore, have better sense than to be tied to the apron strings of a woman who cannot give me an heir. If you," he pointed a finger at his father, "had had the sense to find this out before committing to a marriage, you could have saved me a lot of anguish."

Saved him a lot of anguish? Jhalkaribai was beyond furious with her son. If they had got to know the truth, they could have saved young Sitara all the mental grief and physical torture she had suffered at her son's hands. And now, for the rest of her life she would live with the stigma of a divorce. The Rani felt terribly sorry for her daughter-in-law.

"Even if that was the truth, I think it's still not fair to Sitara. You can't simply send her away just because…"

"Don't you ever listen, Father? Why do you make me repeat every damn thing? Firstly, it's none of your business. Secondly, I think it's unfair to *me*, getting saddled with a barren woman. Let the divorce come through and I'll get married again. But this time round, it will be a woman of my choice."

Jhalkaribai turned to look at her husband, a pathetic expression on her face. He was staring at her as well, a horrified expression on his own. Neither of them could think of a way to stop their son from indulging in this senseless and sadistic behaviour.

They watched on as Harischandra walked out of the room, violently kicking a piece of wooden frame out of his way even as his shoes crunched over the broken glass, far too stunned to say anything.

7

Baroda, 2001

Prince Harshvardhan Singh Gaekwad was twelve going on thirteen when his sister went back to live at the Gaekwad Palace. Having missed her over the twenty-two months when she had been absent from his life, Harshvardhan was thrilled that Sitara had come home for good.

"Sitara *di*!" He hugged her tightly when he met her at dinner time. She had been resting in her room when he had returned from school and their mother Vasundhara Devi had strictly instructed him not to disturb her.

"Harsh." Sitara hugged her young brother, tears pouring down her face as she rubbed her cheek on his head. "You've become so tall."

He moved away to look at her face with a wide grin, only for the excited expression to change into shock when he saw Sitara's tears. "What's wrong, *di*?" he asked, a frown on his young face.

"It's emotion," she said, trying to smile through her tears. "I'm seeing you after almost two years; another six months and I wouldn't have recognised you."

"Why didn't you come before now? And where is *Jijaji*? Is he coming later?" asked Harshvardhan, not really convinced about the reason for her tears. He was intelligent enough to realise they were not exactly tears of joy.

Sitara Devi shook her head slowly, looking up at Vasundhara Devi helplessly. Her brother was still a kid. What could she tell him? Only she seemed to forget that she had herself been barely a child when she got married at the extremely young age of sixteen. Straightening her shoulders, Sitara decided to stick with the truth as far as possible. "Your *Jija* isn't coming."

"Oh! But you will be here for some time at least, *na*? Please say 'yes', *di*." Harshvardhan threw his arms around her once again and hugged her close as if he would never let her go.

Sitara ran her hand over his unruly locks of hair, assuring him, "I'll stay here as long as you want me to."

"Then please don't go away, ever again," said Harshvardhan.

Talk about 'out of the mouths of babes'! Sitara smiled at her brother and said, "As you wish, Harsh."

Two days later, Harshvardhan rushed into his sister's bedroom immediately on returning from school. He wanted Sitara to go riding with Rituraj and himself, just as they used to before she got married. He came to an abrupt halt when he saw her sitting at the window, her shoulders drooped.

"Sitara *di*!"

Sitara wiped her eyes with a lace handkerchief and turned to look at her brother, smiling automatically when she took in his dishevelled appearance, as if he had been in a brawl. "Hello Harsh."

"Why are you crying?"

"I'm not."

He walked closer to her and took her hand in his, the other hand at her chin as he turned her towards him. "You *are* crying! Is it *Jijaji*? Has he upset you?" He was sure of it, that her tears were due to *Yuvaraja* Harischandra Gajanan, her husband. It definitely couldn't be because of any of the Gaekwads. After all, hadn't they all been one happy family for the longest time? Including Rituraj, even if he wasn't a Gaekwad. All before she married and left this palace.

"Harsh!" Sitara shook her head at him. "Just forget it, will you?"

"Why should I? I want to know what happened. I am your brother and the Prince of Gaekwad. I won't hesitate to kill the person who harms you in any way. So, tell me. Did *Yuvaraja* Harischandra Gajanan hurt you in anyway? Tell me, *di*!"

Sitara was startled to note the commanding tone in his young voice, though she couldn't help being touched by it. Getting up from her window seat, she looked at her brother with love overflowing from her heart. "It doesn't matter anymore, Harsh. Your *Jija* is divorcing me and I am finally going to be free of him. He simply doesn't matter anymore."

"Are you sad because he's going to divorce you?" At thirteen, he had an idea what divorce meant. He realised that his sister would be separating from her husband forever. It didn't really matter to him one way or the other as long as she was happy.

Sitara gave her brother a small smile. "No Harsh," she said firmly, "I'm actually glad that he's going to divorce me."

"Are you sure?" he asked, looking into her eyes searchingly. After all, he wanted to be certain that his sister was truly fine.

"I have never been more sure."

"Then you will live here with us forever?" he asked, his young heart fluttering with hope. He had missed his sister terribly. And he knew Rituraj had missed her too.

"If that's what you want, Harsh."

"Yes, I do." He nodded his head vigorously. "Now shall we go for a ride?" he asked, letting go of her hand to rush towards the doorway. "I'll quickly wash and change. I've asked Brijmohan to saddle our horses. And by the way, Rituraj is coming too, just like old times."

"Listen Harsh, I…" Sitara was talking to thin air as her brother had already raced away to his room next door. With a deep sigh, she went to her wardrobe and removed a pair of jodhpurs and a silky top before changing quickly. It was time to move on with her life.

When Sitara lifted her left foot and placed it in the stirrup, she felt two hands at her waist, helping her onto her horse. She was totally startled by the strange sensation she felt as she turned her head to look at Rituraj. This ritual was nothing new. He had always helped her up on her horse and she had taken it for granted in those days. But it looked like she was a different woman now. Sitara was more aware of her body and the sensations that drove her. Well, she had lived as someone's wife all this long, hadn't she? It was probably the reason why she was so aware of Rituraj's touch.

Rituraj was stunned by the shot of powerful current he felt surging through his hands as he lifted Sitara up on her horse. It was an effort not to drop her as his hands tingled with static. Why the hell hadn't he realised it before? It would have saved him and probably her too, a lot of pain. With great difficulty, he wiped away his grimace to concentrate on what she was telling him.

"Thanks, Rituraj," said Sitara in whisper before patting her horse's neck. "Shall we go?" she asked once Harshvardhan and Rituraj had mounted their horses, before taking off at a gallop. It wasn't long before the silver clip holding up her silky hair fell off and she could feel the wind in her tresses as her horse raced beside the other two. For the next hour, Sitara managed to forget that she had ever been married, let alone to the devil incarnate.

Vasundhara Devi smiled through her tears when she saw the three of them—Sitara, Harshvardhan and Rituraj—enter the palace through the side door closest to the stables. Hope fluttered in her heart when she saw her daughter smile for the first time since she had returned to the Gaekwad Palace.

"You have forty-five minutes to bathe and change before dinner is served." Vasundhara Devi greeted the three of them with the words that made it almost seem like old times.

"Race you both," said Harshvardhan, running up the staircase, laughing his head off. "I know I'm going to be first."

"Let's see, brat." Though Rituraj was speaking to Harshvardhan, his eyes were on Sitara's miserable face. He had noticed that her expression had changed once she got off her horse. Probably he would need to encourage her to ride more often if that's what helped her shake off the melancholia which seemed to cover her like a shroud. He realised he simply couldn't stomach watching the princess's sad expression. Was it possible that in this day and age her husband had ill-treated her? That's what his boxing master Vinayak seemed to think. Or was it Harischandra's parents, the Raja and Rani of Indore? Had they behaved badly to their daughter-in-law? The princess he knew used to have an extremely sunny nature. He couldn't remember ever seeing a forlorn expression on her face and he had known her all his life.

Rituraj followed Sitara up the stairs, not commenting on the dejected stoop to her slender shoulders.

On the surface, everything seemed hunky dory during dinner. Raja Manvendra Singh Gaekwad had also joined them, cracking jokes, even managing to bring a few smiles to his daughter's face as they all ate their way through the three-course dinner before tucking into the hot *jalebis* dripping with sugar and ghee.

Sitara pushed her chair back after taking only a small bite of her dessert. "Please excuse me. I'm feeling tired and would like to go to my room."

"Sure," said Vasundhara Devi even as Manvendra Singh nodded his greying head.

"But *di*, it's barely nine-thirty. You can't go to sleep on a full stomach." Harshvardhan raised his voice in protest.

"What do you want to do?" she asked, never having refused her brother anything.

"Shall we play carom? Or maybe cards?"

"Don't you have any homework to complete?" asked Manvendra Singh, looking at his young son with a gentle smile on his face.

Harshvardhan shook his head. "It's Friday, Papa. I don't have school tomorrow," he said gleefully, thrilled to have the whole weekend in front of him.

"Will you play with Rituraj today? I'm really tired Harsh," said Sitara in a cajoling voice.

Harshvardhan looked at his sister's face and saw that she was only speaking the truth. "Will you go riding with us in the morning then?"

"I promise," she said before wishing everyone 'goodnight' and walking towards the staircase.

She had not slept a wink during the three nights she had been at home. How could she when every time she shut her eyes, she felt Harischandra at her side, having his evil way with her? She shuddered whenever she thought of her husband and all the things that he had made her do, and all those things that he had done to her. Rushing into the bathroom, Sitara threw up her dinner violently. It was a while before she managed to get up from her kneeling position on the bathroom floor and washed her face.

Thoroughly beat, Sitara walked over to her bed and lay down, willing desperately for a dreamless sleep. It wasn't long before she got what she wanted and was deeply asleep when Vasundhara Devi went to her room along with a maid who was carrying a glass of hot milk on a silver tray.

The Rani looked down at her sleeping daughter, tears shimmering in her eyes as she gently ran a hand over Sitara's head. Her baby! What must have happened to reduce her to this state? She left after a few minutes, leaving the glass of milk on the table next to the bed. Just in case! Sitara enjoyed her glass of milk in the middle of the night, even if it was lukewarm.

It was 3.45 AM when Harshvardhan woke up with a start. Something had woken him up from deep sleep. As he looked around his room to identify the noise, he heard it again, a scream coming from the direction of Sitara's room. Jumping down from his huge fourposter bed, he ran outside his room and turned left, racing along the corridor until he reached Sitara's bedroom. *Wasn't it a good thing that their doors had been left open?* Or he would have never heard her through the four-foot thick stone wall separating their bedrooms. Harshvardhan rushed to his sister's side as she thrashed about on the bed.

Harshvardhan's stomach churned when he heard his sister's bloodcurdling screams once again at close quarters. Her arms were clutched around her slender body which was curled into a foetus position as she yelled, "Don't beat me, Harry, please don't beat me. I'll do whatever you say. Pleaseeeeeeeeeeeee."

He stood next to her, shaking Sitara's shoulder as he tried to wake her up, even as tears ran down his cheeks. "Sitara *di*, wake up. Wake up *di*. *Jijaji* isn't here to harass you. Don't cry *di*."

Baroda, 2001

Unable to rouse Sitara from her nightmare, a thoroughly shaken Harshvardhan left her to run over to Rituraj's room. "Get up, Rituraj. Please wake up." The young prince shook the older man's shoulder vigorously.

Rituraj woke up with a start, stretching an arm to switch on the bedside lamp, rubbing his sleepy eyes with his other hand. Seeing that it was barely four in the morning, he gave Harshvardhan a startled look, asking, "Is something wrong, Harsh?"

"Come with me. It's Sitara *di*." Harshvardhan was already halfway to the door as he spoke to Rituraj over his shoulder. "She's having a nightmare, I think."

Rituraj pulled on his pyjama jacket and tied the sash around his waist, not bothering with the buttons as he ran behind Harshvardhan, moving faster when he heard Sitara's scream as he stepped into the corridor outside his room.

Rituraj's shocked gaze fell on Harshvardhan who was shaking Sitara awake without any success. She seemed like a woman possessed as she struggled on the bed, screaming her head off, her eyes tightly shut, her eyelashes soaking wet with tears. Thinking on his feet, Rituraj lifted the jug of water on the bedside table and poured half of its contents on Sitara.

Her screaming stopped and she spluttered, making a gurgling noise as she sat up straight, a wild expression in her eyes which were wide open now. "Wha... whatttt?" She stuttered, shaking her head to clear off the water running down her face, as she stared uncomprehendingly at both of them. "What are you two doing here in my room?"

Harshvardhan turned to look up at Rituraj, his gaze an equal mixture of pain and fury.

Rituraj shook his head before going to the bathroom. He fetched a dry towel and gave it to Sitara who didn't seem to be aware that the top half of her body was drenched with water.

She gave him a puzzled look as she took the towel. "Why are you here? I don't need a towel..."

"You do, Sitara. You're wet." Rituraj said in a choked voice, feeling upset and furious to see Sitara in this pathetic state.

"*Di*, do you need help to wipe yourself?" Harsh took the towel from her nerveless fingers and wiped her face gently before patting it over her wet shoulders. "Should I get you another nightdress to wear?"

Rituraj was already on his way to the wardrobe from where he picked up a silk nightdress and placed it at the foot of Sitara's bed, not saying anything.

"But how did I get so wet?" asked Sitara, looking from one to the other as she wiped her hair that was soaked with water.

"*Di*, you were having a nightmare and I couldn't wake you up." Harshvardhan spoke in a rush, a scared expression on his face. "Did you dream of a demon? Was he going to eat you?"

"Demon? Eat me? I..." The colour drained completely from Sitara's face as she recalled her nightmare with crystal clarity. Yes, there had been a demon in her dream. Only he hadn't been eating her, but trying to choke the life out of her. Her eyes met Rituraj's over Harshvardhan's head and she teared up. Burying her face in her hands, Sitara said, "I'm alright now. Why don't you both go to sleep? I'm so sorry that I disturbed you."

"That's okay, *di*. It doesn't matter that we got disturbed. But you were having such a terrible nightmare, I think. Don't you remember anything? You were screaming at the top of your lungs. You..."

Sitara's shocked gaze connected with Rituraj's once again as if to ask him if it was true.

Rituraj gave a small nod. "That's right, Sitara. You were screaming loudly and for a long time, if I'm not mistaken." He was beyond angry with her husband. What the hell had he done to her? It must have been something horrid or she wouldn't be having nightmares for sure, would she?

Sitara pressed the towel against her chest, her heartbeat quickening even as fear raised its ugly head in her. Why couldn't he leave her alone? Hadn't he forsaken her by throwing her out of his life? Then why the hell was he still visiting her in her dreams? She had known in her subconscious that she would meet him in the throes of deep sleep. Which was exactly the reason why she had stayed awake for the last three nights. Was there no escape for her from her demonic husband?

"I think you should both go back to sleep. I'm alright now," she said firmly. What she had undergone during her life with Harischandra was her lookout. She didn't want the other members of her family to worry about her.

"Are you sure, *di*? Or would you like me to call *Mummyji*?" Harshvardhan asked her, reluctant to let go of her hand.

Sitara nodded, striving to give him a reassuring smile. "I'm absolutely sure, Harsh. I'll be fine. It was a stray incident, and hopefully it won't happen again." She had the fingers of both her hands tightly crossed, out of their sight, under the towel.

Harshvardhan's frown disappeared as he leaned forward to give his sister a smacking kiss on her cheek before moving away to give her a sleepy smile. "I'll go then. You sleep well, *di*. Come along Rituraj. I think Sitara *di* will be fine now."

Rituraj let the young prince lead him out of Sitara's bedroom, dragging his footsteps. He could see only too well that she wasn't alright. But he didn't want the young prince to worry unnecessarily. He wished 'goodnight' to Harshvardhan a second time that night, waited for him to settle on his bed before tracing his footsteps back to Sitara's room. He knocked gently on the open door and entered only after he heard her invite him in. He was relieved to see that she had changed out of her wet nightdress and was sitting on the other side of the bed.

"What were you dreaming about, Sitara?" he asked, concern in his voice as he studied her woebegone face minutely.

"Harry, who else?" said Sitara, a bitter note in her voice.

"Do you want to talk about it?" he asked, standing close to her. He didn't feel it was right to sit on the bed next to the princess.

"What's the use, Ritu?" There was abject pain in Sitara's voice as she shut her eyes before burying her face on her raised knees, her arms circling around her bent legs.

Pain squeezed Rituraj's heart. Ritu! That's what she had always called him. He had never believed that he would hear her say that again. "Sitara… listen. You'll feel lighter once you get it off your chest. But no pressure. Only if you really want to talk about it."

She lifted her face from where it was buried, her chin on her knees as she gazed up at Rituraj's concerned face. Maybe she was imagining it but he seemed to have become extremely handsome over the last two years. He had definitely acquired a lot of muscle in that period. "Have you been hitting the gym regularly since I left the palace?" she asked, going off at a tangent.

"Huh?!" Rituraj frowned at her, his mind not really grasping her words as he had been expecting her to tell him about her nightmare.

A glimmer of a smile shone in Sitara's eyes, turning her gaze smoky. "You are way fitter and more muscular than before, Ritu. That's why I asked."

Ruddy colour ran up his slashed cheeks as Rituraj stared at her, thrilled beyond measure that she had noticed. "I'm a trained boxer now."

"Oh!" Sitara's eyes went wide with surprise. The Rituraj she knew was mild by nature. He was more into cricket and tennis than fighting. "And what else have you been learning?" she asked, a teasing note in her voice. It was as if she had forgotten all about what had disturbed her sleep. Though what she was actually doing was trying too hard to push it to the back of her mind by completely changing the subject.

"To shoot. I practise at the shooting range regularly and can use five different kinds of guns and pistols."

"Are you training to be a *Kshatriya*? Did *Bapuji* put you on to this?" she asked, totally astonished by now.

Well, he couldn't very well tell her that he had been taking all his frustrations out in the boxing ring and on the shooting range, could he? He shrugged. "I just wanted to do something different and this also helps me stay fit."

"Shooting does?" she asked, feeling a sudden, mad urge to giggle.

He smiled through his tense and aching facial muscles. He shrugged again. "I enjoy both sports. Anyway, living with a royal family, I could make a suitable bodyguard if need be, couldn't I?"

"Hmm. I suppose you're right. Well then, it's getting late, or rather early morning. Why don't you go to sleep?"

"Are you dismissing me, Princess Sitara Devi?" asked Rituraj, mild sarcasm in his voice. "If you remember, I asked you a question and I'm still waiting for an answer."

Sitara sighed deeply. Why had she even imagined that he would forget it? That just wasn't Rituraj's style.

He was like a dog with a bone and would never ever stray from his target. "What do you want to know?"

"First, about your nightmare. Then, about your life with *Yuvaraja* Gajanan, if you're ready to talk about it."

"You are asking for too much, Rituraj," she said on a sigh.

"Dammit!" he swore. "You are back again to addressing me by my full name." He banged his clenched right fist against the palm of his left hand.

Sitara shook her head at him. "I didn't know you could get angry," she said. The surprising part was that she didn't feel in the least bit scared while she was petrified of Harischandra's temper.

"I didn't know I could either," muttered Rituraj, looking rather shamefaced. "I'm sorry Princess, I…"

"See! You call me Princess and I call you Rituraj. Are we even?" she asked, giving him a small grin.

Rituraj couldn't help the answering smile on his own face. "You are right. That makes us even. So, will you tell me about your nightmare, Sitara?"

"Why don't you pull up a chair and sit down, Ritu?"

Rituraj brought the velvet cushioned ottoman from near her dressing table and sat down next to her bed. "Tell me now."

"Harry was chasing me down a deep, dark tunnel in my dream. I ran as swiftly as I could, but he was gaining on me. I was going to reach the end and there was no way to escape. I…" Sitara stopped midway, her throating clogging with fear, a faraway expression in her gaze as she stared at nothing, obviously recalling her nightmare.

"Why would it matter? He's your husband, after all. Wouldn't it be a nice thing if he caught up with you?" Rituraj hated himself for saying those words, but it must be true, right? Why would she not want to be caught by her husband? After all, it wasn't as if Sitara had sought to divorce him. It was Harischandra who planned to divorce his wife.

"Nice?" Sitara threw back her head and gave a humourless laugh. "It would be anything but nice. You don't know Harry, Ritu…"

"So, tell me, Sitara. Was he nice to you? Did you have a good marriage? Are you terribly hurt now that he wants to divorce you?" Rituraj felt as if he was digging deep into his own flesh to remove a stray bullet as he asked her those questions. But then, he had to know. He had to know how upset she was now that her husband had sent her back home to her parents.

"Nice?" There was abject bitterness in Sitara's voice. "Harry doesn't know the meaning of words such as 'nice' or 'kind'," she said, lifting her hands to draw quotation marks in the air. "He is the devil incarnate. Beating me with a stick was the mildest thing he did to me. I…"

Rituraj jumped up, knocking the ottoman on its side in his fury. "What the hell are you saying? Did your husband beat you? Really? Assault the Princess of Gaekwad? How DARE he?" He was yelling by now, not really caring that he might wake up all the inhabitants of the entire palace. "Does Rani *ma* even know about it?"

"Hush Ritu. Stop shouting. You don't want *Mummyji* and *Bapuji* to come up here, do you?" Sitara frowned at him, even as her heart picked up its beat.

She couldn't help but feel good that he was ready to take up the cudgels on her behalf.

"But why did you put up with it, Sitara? That too, for twenty-two months! You should have come home immediately. Why the hell did you wait for him to send you home? I am going to kill the bastard," Rituraj snarled. While he had reduced the volume, the anger in his voice had magnified all the more.

"Calm down, Ritu. I thought you wanted to know the reason for my nightmare? Or doesn't it interest you anymore?" She was keen to shed the burden she had been carrying for almost two years. In reality it felt like a lifetime. And who better than her best friend Rituraj?

Rituraj took a deep breath which didn't really help him calm down. But deferring to her words, he lifted the fallen ottoman and set it straight before sitting on it. "Tell me everything." He sat closer to her cot, keeping his bunched-up fists out of her sight.

9

Indore, 1999

Sitara and Harischandra had not celebrated their wedding night since it had been late when they reached Indore and the *Yuvaraja* had claimed that he was exhausted. Sitara had a bedroom of her own adjoining her husband's. She had gone to sleep the moment her head touched her pillow, too young and innocent to be concerned that her wedding hadn't been consummated.

The next evening, a palace maid helped Sitara deck up for her first night with her husband. The thirty-year-old Rabri had been working at the Gajanan Palace since she was a kid. Sitara couldn't see that the maid was jealous of the new bride. Having been bedded by Harischandra whenever the fancy took him, Rabri had begun to consider the prince as her property. Now that he had married a teenager and brought the bride back home had left a bitter after taste in the servant's mouth. The bile turned to poison when Rabri set her eyes on the beautiful and ethereal Sitara Devi.

How the hell can this young chit satisfy the appetites of a virile man like the Yuvaraja? Rabri was genuinely flummoxed. Running the hair brush through the princess's dark and curly locks a tad too roughly,

Rabri eyed the younger woman via the floor length mirror set in her bedroom, frowning at the shape of her nubile breasts and slim limbs as she sat on the chair in her undergarments. No! Sitara Devi could definitely not please the *Yuvaraja*. Rabri knew for a fact he liked voluptuous women. With a snide smile on her face, she plaited Sitara's hair neatly before helping her into the silk and lace *gaghra choli* in gold colour. She refused to acknowledge the fact that Sitara glowed in her new attire, her skin gleaming in the light of the bright chandelier that hung from the ceiling of her room.

"*Chalo, Yuvarani*! You sit back and relax until the *Yuvaraja* joins you here. I hope for your sake that you have it in you to make him happy. He is a man of great needs."

Sitara Devi looked at Rabri through the mirror, a dark eyebrow up in query. Wasn't the servant being a little too familiar? The princess gave the other woman a haughty look freezing Rabri into silence. Knowing she had outstepped her rank in a moment of ridiculous jealousy, the maid beat a swift retreat and said, "If you will excuse me, Princess Sitara Devi, I have to tend to the Rani."

"You may go," said Sitara, regal to the core, unaware of how she was making Rabri burn from anger within.

More than an hour later Harischandra walked into Sitara's bedchamber, without bothering to knock, clad in a luxurious silk dressing gown.

Sitara jumped off the bed to stare at her bridegroom, conceding that he looked even more handsome and suave than yesterday when they had tied the knot.

"Good evening, my dear Sitara," said Harischandra, walking up to her and pulling her into his arms.

"Sss!" Sitara couldn't stop the protest that left her lips when she felt his arms holding her slender body in too tight a grip.

"What?" he laughed loudly, tightening his grip even more, "Don't tell me you are too delicate, my princess?"

Sitara clammed up. No, she wasn't going to tell him that. He was her husband and her mother had told her clearly that it was her duty to please him. Okay, maybe it hurt some, but what did it matter? It seemed to give him pleasure, didn't it?

"Look at me," he ordered.

Sitara lifted her face up to his, looking shyly into his steely grey eyes and was startled to see the lust burning there. Though barely sixteen, she understood enough to know the difference between love and lust. What she saw in his eyes brought fear to her heart, instead of the joy she had expected. What was he going to do to her?

"Are you afraid of me?" he asked, running his gaze over her delicate features. *What the hell had my parents seen in her that they believed she would make me a perfect wife*? She just didn't seem his type, at all.

Sitara Devi straightened her shoulders. Afraid? Never! The Gaekwad princess didn't know the meaning of fear. She looked her husband straight in his eyes as she shook her head, saying firmly, "No, I'm not."

Harischandra threw back his head and laughed uproariously. Neither of them was aware Rabri was standing outside the partly open door and was listening, gritting her teeth when she heard the *Yuvaraja* laugh. Had the princess already managed to ensnare the new husband in her seductive net?

Harischandra studied his young wife's face. She did look unafraid, and too damn innocent. And that's what set his blood roaring in his head. The debauched prince found her innocence grating on his nerves. Pulling her face up to his, he kissed her hard, grinding his teeth against her lips, excited when he drew blood.

Sitara teared up, unused to physical pain of any kind. She stood still, even when her body clamoured to escape Harischandra's hold.

Harischandra lifted his head to look down at his wife, a wide grin on his face. Sitara opened her eyes to look at him boldly, only for her eyes to go wide in horror when she noticed the blood smeared on his lips and teeth. Bestial! That was the word which came to her shocked mind.

"You excite me, my pretty princess!" said Harischandra, removing his arms from his wife before pulling his dressing gown off his body. "Go on, get undressed," he ordered, giving her a sly look.

Sitara stared at his naked body in morbid fascination. It wasn't as if she was unfamiliar with the parts of a male body, having seen her brother naked till he turned all of five years, at which point Harshvardhan had been given strict instructions by Vasundhara Devi not to run around in the nude. But there was a world of difference between the body parts of a five-year-old boy and a twenty-eight-year-old man. Harischandra was fit, his body whipcord straight.

Her gaze slid down his body before coming to rest on the organ declaring he was a man, her eyes growing wider by the minute. It looked like a beast unleashed, twitching and turning, as if clamouring for release. Sitara swiftly lifted her gaze up to his face, her arms crossed over her upper body in a gesture of protection.

"What? Do I excite you?" he asked, continuing to grin at her. "Can you undress yourself or do you need help?"

Sitara gave him a small nod and immediately shook her head, indicating that she didn't need help, making him laugh once again, which in turn angered the eavesdropping Rabri. Well, Sitara definitely didn't want help from her husband to undress herself.

But her hands trembled as she reached for the diamond brooch that held her crepe *dupatta* on her left shoulder, the pin leaving a tear in the material as she removed it.

"Tch! I think you need help," declared Harischandra, before turning towards the door and calling, "Rabri, come here!"

A visibly gleeful Rabri walked into the princess's bedroom, shocking Sitara to the core. What was the maid doing here on the royal couple's wedding night? That too with her husband standing buck naked in the middle of the room?

"Er…"

Harischandra ignored his wife as he ordered the maid, "Help my wife out of her clothes."

"*Ji Yuvaraja*," said Rabri, her greedy eyes running over his naked form lustily, even as she walked towards the princess. Her hands were anything but gentle as she removed the knots at the back of the long blouse that the princess wore, her eyes still on the prince.

Hot colour ran up Sitara Devi's face as she turned to give Rabri a fiery look before looking at her husband who was actually gazing at the maid, his tongue flicking wetly over his lips. Confused, but thoroughly irritated about the maid invading their privacy, Sitara said, "That will do, Rabri. You may leave."

Harischandra threw back his head and laughed yet again, as if his wife had cracked a hilarious joke. What was worse was when Rabri's tinkling laughter joined his, even as she continued helping Sitara out of her clothes.

"You heard me. Leave! Now!" Sitara raised her voice by a few decibels to give the order even as she moved away from the servant.

"Come on, Sitara. You must allow Rabri to help you. She's good at what she's doing and she'll also help you feel more comfortable," said Harischandra, walking towards the two women.

Sitara lifted her startled gaze to his when he brought both his hands forward, his right hand squeezing her left breast. Ignoring the pain, she looked down to see what he was doing with his left hand when she didn't feel it against her body and was completely revolted when she saw it was curled on another breast, one that was bigger, plumper and a few shades darker than her own. Her husband was making love to not only his new wife, but also the Gajanan Palace maid, it seemed.

And that's how her married life began, with Harischandra introducing Sitara to a threesome in her marital bed. He gave her no choice but to watch them as he made torrid love to Rabri.

Within a couple of weeks, the *Yuvaraja*, with a lot of coercion, both with his sharp tongue and even sharper hand that didn't hesitate to lift in a beating, had trained Sitara to make love not just to him, but to Rabri too.

Sitara was far too shell-shocked and humiliated to utter a word to anyone about it. But then, who could she talk to? She couldn't very well tell her parents-in-law about what she was undergoing under their own roof. After all, it was their son who was perpetrating this horror. Why would they take her side?

After losing her virginity and having been subjected to the degrading treatment under the *Yuvaraja* and his maid's hands, Sitara ran to the bathroom and threw up. It finally dawned on her why Rabri had seemed angry while decking her up for her first night. The maid had been jealous of Harischandra's new bride.

Now she had no reason to be! Rabri continued to be Harischandra's plaything in bed. It was just that he had got the maid another new toy.

Sitara threw up once again, her skin crawling as she dragged herself under the shower. Was she glad that she had her own room! But sleep refused to come as she lay on her bed, staring at the high ceiling, unable to find a way out of the situation.

The humiliation continued and seemed to get worse each night. Sitara's body became desensitized to the physical violence that she underwent at Harischandra's hands. It began playfully with him slapping her bottom during sex. One day, she almost fainted when he hit her across her face, his excitement increasing manifold when he heard her inadvertent scream. At times, it wasn't just Harischandra who beat Sitara. Rabri was given complete license to treat his wife as she pleased, many times egged on by Harischandra.

Soon, cigar burn marks, blood clots, even open wounds became regular features on Sitara's body. She learned to cover up most of them, except for the blemishes left on her face. Even those, she often concealed under the cover of heavy makeup. But there was the one time when her mother-in-law noticed it. It was also when Sitara was running a temperature. She almost always tried to blank out her mind but her body protested with each new perversion and physical atrocity her husband inflicted on her.

What irritated Harischandra the most was his wife's stoic behaviour. Sitara, who had screamed the first couple of times, had stopped making any noise, whatever he did. She put up with everything he doled out to her, without reacting in anyway. And that's what bugged him, making him all the more violent.

Seeing his anger against his wife, Rabri was only too happy to encourage him to mistreat Princess Sitara all the more. Between the two of them, they did their best to make Sitara's life purgatory.

While Sitara could feel the fires of hell, she refused to succumb and continued to maintain a calm demeanour. In a way, it gave her tremendous strength to stump the two of them. And she was fairly conscious of what her behaviour bordering on cold was doing to the *Yuvaraja*.

Well, wasn't she a princess?! She did have her dignity to maintain.

10

Indore, 2001

Harischandra Gajanan was having a drink with a doctor friend at the latter's residence. Another debauched son of a bitch, Dr. Amarnath Jadhav was a gynaecologist who was infamous for his malpractices.

"I don't understand this, Amar. It has been eighteen months since I married Sitara and I've never used protection. Why the hell is the woman not getting pregnant?" There was a heavy frown on Harischandra's face as he tilted his head back to pour the glass of premium whisky down his throat.

"Do you try your usual shenanigans on your wife, Harry?" Amarnath gave his friend a sly grin as he asked the question.

Harischandra lifted a supercilious brow at his friend, even as he grinned back. "Whatever do you mean by that?"

"You very well know what I mean. Do you beat her up during sex?" Amarnath asked outright.

"Of course I do, you bastard, not that it's any of your business." Harischandra was quick to anger. Amarnath was a friend. But that still didn't give him a right to talk about Harischandra's relationship with his wife.

"You just made it mine, Harry. Will you calm down?" said Amarnath, getting up to refill their glasses. "I wasn't trying to read you a moral lecture, you idiot. I was asking you a genuine question."

Harischandra took the glass the other man offered, continuing to scowl viciously at him. "And what was your question?"

"If you beat up your wife during sex." Amarnath lifted a hand to stop Harischandra from interrupting him as he continued, "Sometimes, you see, physical abuse makes people clam up. Maybe Sitara Devi is unable to get pregnant because she's being treated with violence."

"Did you study medicine or witchcraft?" asked Harischandra, heavy sarcasm in his voice.

Amarnath shrugged. "The psyche plays a huge role in the way a physical body behaves and that's the truth. It's one of the subjects every doctor studies, though rarely uses in treatments unless the doctor goes on to become a psychiatrist. What I would advise you, since you asked, is that you should stop the violence and give it a few months. If she still doesn't get pregnant, you should have a thorough medical check-up done on her."

Harischandra nodded slowly, thinking hard. It wasn't only his parents who had asked him a few times about Sitara not getting pregnant. Even he had been getting a little bothered about it. He had sex with her, almost every night. Sometimes, even during the day. And well, the violence factor had only upped with each passing day. But then, what was he to do?

The lack of fear in his wife only made him more savage in his treatment of her.

"So, you think I should stop the violence altogether?"

"Yes. Chances are high that she would get pregnant soon. After all, I have great faith in your prowess." Amarnath laughed.

Harischandra laughed along with his friend, thoroughly flattered. "So do I!" he agreed, chuckling.

Sitara was surprised when Rabri abruptly stopped coming to her room. She didn't think too much about it as she was tremendously relieved. Then quite unexpectedly even her husband stopped beating her or burning her with his cigar. Once the brutality and the third person were taken out of the bedroom, the sex with Harischandra was not all that bad. Well, Sitara mentally shrugged to herself, she didn't know if it was good sex or bad sex. Just that it was less painful and more tolerable.

As for the fear, while she had pretended to be courageous, young Sitara had been cowering inside all the time. It had been an effort to stop her teeth from chattering and her whole body from trembling every time Harishchandra or Rabri entered her bedroom. But it had helped, her stubborn nature. She had managed to control her body's reactions and present a brave front. Her silent rebellion continuously irked her husband and it was the only thing which helped her get from one day to the next.

And she continued to retain her dispassionate expression whenever he was around. After all, Harischandra had never bothered to befriend his wife and ended up treating her like an object meant for his pleasure. He hadn't acknowledged her as a fellow human being with a mind and heart of her own. He didn't even know how intelligent his wife was. Why should she give him any respect at all? She was married to him and had conjugal duties towards him. Her job ended there. And Sitara refused to look at long term consequences. For somebody who had just turned seventeen, it wasn't an easy life. Sitara Devi, true to her royal lineage, managed to retain her dignity even under these bizarre circumstances.

It went on for three more months before Harischandra asked her one morning, "Do you get your periods regularly?"

What kind of a question was that? Those were the days when she was free of his attention. It had become a habit for the married Sitara to eagerly await her periods each month. She gave him a nod, saying, "Yes, Harry, I do."

"Which means you aren't pregnant." There was a heavy frown as he eyed her slender form. *Has she lost more weight*? He couldn't help but notice that Sitara had been steadily losing weight since she married him. He had better tackle his mother about it. Were they feeding her at all? It didn't strike Harischandra that his wife's appetite had been nil since she went to live at the Gajanan Palace as his bitter half.

Sitara didn't respond to his comment. Of course, it meant she wasn't pregnant. Why was he stating the obvious? Whatever else he was, Harischandra was definitely not stupid.

"Get ready. We are going to see a gynaecologist."

Sitara got up immediately to obey him, without question. But her mind ran around in circles. Why did he want to take her to a gynaecologist? Wasn't it a good thing that she hadn't got pregnant? Sitara definitely didn't want to mother her monster husband's child. But then, her not getting pregnant was more due to luck than any protection either of them had used. Maybe it was a good thing to visit a gynaecologist. What in case something was drastically wrong with her? With her uterus? The joke was neither husband nor wife thought something could be wrong with Harischandra. If a lady didn't get pregnant, it was she who was the culprit.

Patriarchy at its zenith!

She quickly wore a chiffon sari and minimal jewellery before thrusting her feet into a pair of leather sandals. Sitara had somehow managed to convince Rabri she didn't require the maid's help to get ready. She couldn't stomach the other woman's touch. What happened in bed was a different thing altogether—something over which Sitara had no control. But out of bed, the princess was clear about what she wanted and what she didn't.

Dr. Amarnath Jadhav had recommended a lady doctor at Harischandra's behest. The *Yuvaraja* managed to get an immediate appointment with Dr. Vidhya Shukla.

"Namaste, Yuvaraja, Yuvarani!" The gynaecologist greeted the royal couple with folded hands, sitting down in her chair only after they were seated comfortably.

Harischandra did most of the talking, telling the doctor about their marriage and sex life, not mentioning the violence quotient.

After listening to his monologue without interrupting him, the doctor got up to examine Sitara, asking her to lie down on the couch. Harischandra insisted on being present during the examination, determined to be in complete control.

After doing a basic check-up, Dr. Shukla spoke to Harischandra. "Sitara ma'am will need to get admitted in the nursing home for two-three days and undergo a number of tests before I can arrive at a conclusion."

Harischandra looked at the doctor thoughtfully, a heavy frown on his face. While he enjoyed his reputation for being violent, he still didn't like the idea of the doctor discovering all the marks he had inflicted on his wife. And the damn woman's skin was too freaking sensitive, turning black and blue all the time. "We will think it over and get back to you," he said in response to Vidhya's words.

Vidhya nodded her head, before taking her prescription pad and writing out a few vitamin pills. Addressing Sitara, she said, "You can take these supplements for the next three months and come back whenever you wish."

Sitara gave her a nod, not saying anything. Who cared about her opinion anyway? She would be doing exactly what Harischandra wanted her to do.

Harischandra walked out of the clinic in a foul temper, not bothering to see if his wife was following him.

Once they got back to the palace, he ranted and raved at his mother as if it was all her fault that her daughter-in-law wasn't able to conceive. Jhalkaribai listened patiently to all his complaints, a calm expression on her face. As the queen, she had her spies in the palace and was aware of Sitara's life with her son—how it had been three months back and how it had improved since then. She refrained from giving her opinion, only because she knew for a fact that her son would never listen to her.

"What? Don't you have anything to say? What kind of a mother are you? Don't you care that my wife is unable to produce a *waaris* for our kingdom?" Harischandra yelled at his mother.

Jhalkaribai finally opened her mouth to say, "Why don't you follow the doctor's advice and admit Sitara in the nursing home? Let's find out what the issue is, if there's one in the first place."

Harischandra visibly calmed down. "I think I'll do just that. Sitara, let's get you admitted first thing tomorrow."

Sitara nodded politely, not really concerned about the medical expedition. She was just enormously relieved to be away from the palace and away from this manic sadist for a few days. She gave a shrug mentally. Maybe she could treat it as a holiday!

And a break from monotony it turned out to be, her stay at the high-end nursing home with its 5-star facilities. Princess Sitara Devi Gajanan had a suite to herself, the best available, with nurses waiting on her hand and foot. The sheer joy of knowing that she didn't have to meet a single soul from the Gajanan Palace for three whole days, was the closest to bliss that Sitara had experienced in her young life. Well, at least after she got married.

Okay, they poked and prodded her a bit as that was the reason she was here at the nursing home. But then, it was nothing compared to the torture she regularly underwent at Harischandra's hands. She even slept well during the nights.

At the end of the three-day stay, Dr. Vidhya Shukla pronounced her a one hundred per cent fit to be a mother.

No! *Yuvaraja* Harischandra Gajanan was not at all happy with the test results. If what Dr. Vidhya said was true, then how come Sitara wasn't pregnant by now?

"Why don't you get yourself tested, Harry?" Amarnath asked his friend when they met up in the evening a few days later.

"Shut up, Amar. Unless you want me to kill you," said Harischandra, glaring at the other man. It was with a great effort he stopped himself from slapping Amarnath. But then, Harischandra showed his strength only against those weaker than him. He knew for a fact that Amarnath would simply hit him back if provoked and he wasn't keen on fighting his strong friend.

"Listen, I'm not saying anything major might be wrong with you. But we'll know better once we have the test results. You can probably take a mild treatment that will help you father a dozen kids."

"I won't repeat myself after this. SHUT THE FUCK UP, AMAR!" Harischandra hurled his glass at the empty stone grate where it shattered to a million pieces. "Screw you, you bastard! With a friend like you, I don't need an enemy." He got up abruptly to walk out of Amarnath's home, too angry to be pacified.

Harischandra didn't sleep the whole night as he paced on the veranda outside his bedroom. Something was amiss! That much was definitely true. And no way could it be that he wasn't virile enough to father a child. While medical tests had said Sitara was fit for motherhood, Harischandra came to the conclusion that something must be drastically wrong with his wife. Maybe it was the fact that she was too young. Her uterus must be weak. That must be it. He was going to be thirty in a month. It was high time he became a father. If Sitara couldn't give him his heir, then she was unfit to be his wife.

Harischandra snapped his fingers, his meandering thoughts collating into a vicious idea. He would divorce her. Anyway, she was useless as a wife as she was completely timid in bed. While he needed a lioness, someone like Rabri. It was sad Rabri was a maid. Otherwise, he could have made her his wife.

It never struck Harischandra that he hadn't managed to get the maid pregnant in all these years. But then, logic wasn't exactly his strong point.

It was past five in the morning when he arrived at the conclusion that he would divorce Sitara. Finally at peace, Harischandra went to sleep and woke up only at lunchtime.

Getting up, he went directly in search of Sitara. Walking into her room, where she was reading at her desk, he announced baldly, "I'm going to divorce you."

Sitara lifted her head to look at her husband as he towered over her. Had she heard him right? "What?" she asked in a small voice.

"You heard me. Pack your bags immediately. I'm planning to call your father. Let him come and take you back home." He did an about turn and walked out of her room.

Sitara stared at the closed door, stunned. Had her husband really mentioned the D word? Seriously? A wild grin broke out on her face as she got up from her chair and did a pirouette on the balls of her feet before falling down face first on the floor as her head whirled.

She didn't care as she lay there on the carpet, laughter and tears vying with each other as she tried to visualise a life without her demonical husband. The thought brought her untold joy.

Baroda, 2001

By the time Sitara came to the end of her story, Rituraj was holding her hands tightly in his, trying to absorb her pain, wishing he could help her heal instantaneously. It was obvious that she had given him the barest outlines of the terribly dark two years with Gajanan. But he could read between the lines fairly well.

He couldn't digest the fact that her parents and he, Rituraj, her best friend, had been eating well and sleeping peacefully, having no idea whatsoever of the princess's suffering. She was so young, dammit! Only a teenager. How could her husband treat her so terribly? And what had his parents been doing? Or were they as devilish as Harischandra himself?

How he wished he could take them all to court! The whole royal family of Gajanans! But it would all backfire, dragging the Gaekwad name through mud as well. Shit! What a snarl!

He gently stroked the back of Sitara's hands with his thumbs, hoping against hope that now finally her mind would be at peace. She had by a sheer stroke of luck escaped from her husband's clutches on her person. But Gajanan still seemed to rule her mind. Or why would she get such terrible dreams?

"Is this the first time you had a nightmare?" he asked her in a whisper.

Sitara shook her head, replying in a hoarse voice, "I keep getting them on and off. But it's the first time after I returned home."

"I think it's best you see a doctor," he said, moving away from her as the urge to pull her into his arms became too much to bear.

Sitara felt bereft when he walked away. Rituraj's presence had helped to keep the pain at bay. And the anger in his eyes as he heard her pathetic story had helped too. "I don't know Ritu. Let's wait and watch. Maybe they won't come again now that I have got everything off my chest." She gave him a small smile. "You are a good listener."

He gave her a nod in return, his face hard and unsmiling. "I still want to kill your husband, slowly and painfully!"

She gave a soft laugh. "Please don't bother. I know it'll rid the world of the devil, but I don't want you languishing in jail."

Rituraj gave a long sigh which shuddered from the depths of his being. How he wished that he could make her his, and protect her till the end of their lives! But then if wishes were horses, this beggar would ride, wouldn't he?

"You must rest, Sitara. I'll go." He walked towards the doorway.

"Ritu!"

He turned and looked at her over his shoulder, an eyebrow up in query. No! He would not walk back to her or he might never leave. Just now, Rituraj didn't feel very strong.

"Don't tell *Mummyji* and *Bapuji* anything, okay?"

He sighed again. He had so hoped that she wouldn't lay down this condition. But Sitara knew him only too well, it seemed.

"Are you certain, Sitara? Isn't it better that your parents know?"

She shook her head firmly. "I don't want them to feel ashamed of me."

He walked swiftly back to her, taking her chin firmly in his hand and lifting her face to his. "Don't be silly, Sitara. Why would they be ashamed of you? It's Harischandra's parents who should be embarrassed of him."

"Promise me, Ritu," she insisted, stretching her right palm up to him.

He placed his own on it and said, "Okay, I promise," not liking it one bit. Even as he walked out of her room, he was wondering how he could break his word to her.

The decision was completely taken out of both their hands when Harshvardhan arrived at the dining table for breakfast. "How are you, *di*?" asked the young prince in his bell-like voice. "Have you completely recovered from your nightmare? Did you sleep well after that?"

Vasundhara Devi's spoon clattered on the table next to her plate as she turned to her daughter, even as Manvendra Singh threw the newspaper down before giving Sitara his complete attention. Rituraj couldn't help the small smile which flitted on his face as he also looked at Sitara.

"What happened Sitara?" Manvendra Singh asked her. "You didn't say anything about a nightmare, *beta*."

"It's nothing major, *Bapuji*. I was only dreaming…"

"Sitara *di* was screaming terribly, *Bapuji*. So loudly that I could hear her in my room. I couldn't wake her up. I took Rituraj's help and he had to throw a jug of water over *di* to make her wake up from her bad dream." Harshvardhan explained everything in explicit detail to his parents.

Vasundhara Devi met her husband's worried eyes before turning to her daughter again. "What were you dreaming about, Sitara?"

Sitara sighed. "As I said, it was nothing…"

"…major. Yes, I heard you. But if it wasn't anything big, why wouldn't you get up when Harsh tried to wake you?" Manvendra Singh pinned his daughter with his sharp gaze.

Sitara lost the little appetite that she had. "I don't want you and *Mummyji* to feel bad, *Bapuji*. But I didn't have a very nice life with Harry." Her voice was a whisper when she uttered those words.

"Meaning?" Manvendra Singh's voice was stern.

"Her husband is a sadistic brute." Rituraj couldn't control himself as he burst out.

Manvendra Singh turned to look at Rituraj while Sitara glared at her friend, her eyes accusing.

"I'm sorry, Sitara. I can't keep quiet anymore. And you have to admit that I did keep my promise. You can't blame me if Harsh decided to talk about your nightmare. And I'm glad you did, Harsh." Rituraj turned to address Manvendra Singh, "*Rajaji*, I think Sitara should see a doctor. She has undergone vile abuse at her husband's hands, both physical and mental. And I think we should probably thank our lucky stars the man decided to divorce her, instead of feeling bad about it."

The Raja and Rani of Gaekwad had always treated him like family and Rituraj had no qualms about giving his opinion when required. And if it was in any way going to improve Sitara's sorry life, then he wasn't going to keep quiet about it.

Vasundhara Devi took her daughter's thin hand in hers, tears shimmering in her eyes. "What did he do to you, my *bachcha*? Why did you never tell us anything?"

Manvendra Singh wanted to break something. It spoke of the measure of control he had over his temper that he didn't do anything as he sat back in his chair, his hands clenched into fists.

Harshvardhan got up after he finished breakfast, the trauma of the night not having affected his appetite in any way. "Rituraj, *di*, shall we go for a ride after you finish your breakfast?"

Sitara smiled at her young brother. "Yes, Harsh. Let's go in an hour."

"Right. I'll go finish my homework by the time you guys are ready. See you all." He left.

"Let me call Kanjilal home," said Manvendra Singh. Dr. Kanjilal Trivedi was the third-generation physician to the royal house of Gaekwads, his grandfather and later his father, having treated four generations of Manvendra's family.

The four of them finished their breakfast in a desultory fashion, not saying much, before Rituraj called the doctor at Manvendra Singh's instructions and invited him over to the palace in the evening. It didn't matter that it was Saturday evening. The doctor was extremely loyal to the family and always ready to serve them whenever needed.

Kanjilal was plump and jovial, cracking jokes constantly, not really bothered if anyone laughed at them or not.

"Hello, Sitara, my dear! How have you been? You have forgotten all of us after going to live with your husband, it seems," he greeted the princess of Gaekwad.

Sitara gave the doctor a half smile that didn't quite reach her eyes. "It's nothing like that, uncle. I…"

"Sitara has been suffering abuse at her husband's hands, Kanji. I want you to check her thoroughly," said Manvendra Singh in a stern voice. The Raja had insisted on Rituraj telling him everything and the latter had been only too glad to get it all off his chest. Only the violence, of course. He decided that it was not on his part to tell the Raja about Sitara's sex life with her husband. In any case, Dr. Kanjilal Trivedi was only a general physician.

"What?" The laughter disappeared from Kanjilal's face as he looked at both father and daughter in turn. "What happened, Sitara?" he asked in a mild voice. "I think I should talk to Sitara in private," said the doctor, looking at the others.

Sitara got up to lead the doctor to the library and not really having a choice, she told him briefly about the violence she had suffered at Harischandra's hands.

Kanjilal spoke to her long, asking many questions as he was keen to know the cause of her nightmares. Having brought Sitara into the world and also being close to the royal family, he knew for a fact that the Gaekwad princess was a brave young woman. That she had succumbed to nightmares bespoke of something more than beatings.

Sitara answered the doctor's questions in a choked voice, unable to refute him when the doctor asked her directly if she had suffered from sexual violation. Even then, she admitted to it in a few words, not sharing too many details. Even with Rituraj, she hadn't told him everything. All said and done, Rituraj was barely a year older than her. She didn't want to shock him by speaking about all of Harischandra's atrocities.

It was an hour and a half later when Kanjilal finally got up from the comfortable armchair he was ensconced in, indicating the interview was finally over. "You need to see a psychiatrist," he declared.

"Of course I don't, Kanji Uncle," protested Sitara, her eyes wide as she looked into his kind face.

"Let me talk to your father before we take a call on it," he said pacifyingly, walking out into the marble-floored hall. It was obvious that the others were waiting anxiously for them.

Rituraj jumped to his feet even before Manvendra said anything, gesturing for the doctor to sit down on the adjacent sofa. "What's your verdict, Kanjilal?" asked the Raja in an expressionless voice.

"Sitara has suffered a lot of trauma, both physical and mental, at her husband's hands. While the physical scars will fade away in the next few months, we cannot say the same about the mental scars, which must be the reason for her nightmares. And if what she says is true, Sitara has been having them for a long time. I would suggest that the best way to deal with this is to consult a psychiatrist." He lifted a hand when Vasundhara Devi would have interrupted. "Let me finish. If you feel hesitant about sending her to a consultant in Baroda, I can suggest one from some other state or even in another country."

Vasundhara Devi was on the verge of tears since she still wasn't clear about what her daughter had suffered through. And now it looked like they would be living with both; the shame of their daughter's divorce and her treatment by a psychiatrist. However modern one's outlook was, going to a psychiatrist still implied Sitara was either a lunatic or insane. While it was true that it was the beginning of the new millennium, people could still be quite backward in their thoughts. Hugging her daughter close, she gave her husband an anxious look.

"Rani Vasundhara Devi, you were going to say?" The doctor prompted Sitara's mother.

Vasundhara shook her head. "No, you answered all my questions even before I asked you, Kanjilal."

Manvendra Singh spoke, "If that's the only solution, then we have no choice but to go with it. It's best if the treatment takes place somewhere abroad, Kanji. Where would you suggest?"

"I know this doctor in London. In fact, I have sent a few cases to Dr. Gerard King over the years. Every patient has returned, completely cured. If you are alright with it, I will call the doctor and speak to him on your behalf and find out if he's free to take on

Sitara's case. What do you say, Manvendra*ji*?" Kanjilal addressed the Raja.

Manvendra Singh looked at his wife who gave a small nod, before turning to speak to Kanjilal. "We will go with your advice, Kanjilal."

"Good. In that case, let me take your leave. I'll talk to Dr. King tonight and will inform you tomorrow."

"You must have dinner with us," said Vasundhara Devi.

"Yes, I also insist," said Manvendra Singh, getting up. "It's way past dinner time, anyway. Come along."

Late at night, Vasundhara Devi spoke to her husband in an anxious voice. "How can we simply leave everything and go to London for six months, Manu? And we cannot send Sitara alone. The poor child has already suffered so much without having a soul she could confide in." Her voice wobbled as she made a valiant effort to stop her eyes from overflowing.

"You are right, Vasundhara. I have been thinking of the same thing. Sitara cannot go alone. Why don't we send Rituraj with her? For one, he's a trained boxer and sharpshooter. He will make a perfect bodyguard and escort for Sitara. And we can trust him to take care of her as well."

"Are you sure?" The Rani had her own misgivings. She had noticed the way Rituraj had almost fallen apart after Sitara's wedding. Would it be fair to send the two of them alone to London? Wouldn't it be too much pressure on the young man who was nursing a broken heart? Not that she was worried that Rituraj would turn the situation to his advantage in any way. She would trust the boy with her life.

Manvendra Singh looked at his wife and said, "Do we really have a choice? We'll all of us go to London on the pretext of a holiday and settle the two of them in a comfortable rented apartment before returning home. That would be for the best."

"Do you think Harischandra would create any kind of trouble?"

"He wouldn't dare!" Manvendra Singh's calm face had turned red with temper, his dark eyes glowing fierily in the lamplight. "I will have him arrested if he gets within a few feet of our daughter. Which is also the reason why I want Rituraj to go with her. I know for a fact he will protect her with his life."

She nodded, in full agreement with her husband. "I just pray to God that Sitara becomes normal again."

Manvendra Singh's shoulders sagged as he sat down on his side of the bed and buried his face in his hands. "I sincerely hope so too," he said in a broken voice.

The Raja and Rani of Gaekwad aged twenty years overnight, the angst about their darling daughter eating into them.

12

Mandvi, 2018

"Sitara!"

She looked up from the file she was studying to see Rituraj standing before her and gave him a royal nod. "Tell me, Rituraj."

"Prince Rajvardhan Thakore of Udaipur called me. He would like an appointment with you."

A small frown pleated Sitara's neat forehead. What did the prince of Udaipur want to see her about? She had heard his name, of course. But she didn't know much about him. Actually, after her horrific marriage and divorce Sitara Devi pretty much kept to herself. "What does he want to see me about?" she asked her once-upon-a-time friend and Man Friday.

"He insists that he can share that only with you. And he also mentioned it was a matter of pressing importance. He promised not to take more than half an hour of your time."

Sitara pressed an index finger on her lips, inadvertently drawing Rituraj's gaze to their lusciousness, making his body spring to attention. Only she remained totally unaware of the effect she was having on him. A thoughtful expression on her face, she lifted her gaze up to his and said, "Okay, invite him over."

At present, the thirty-five-year-old princess was stationed at their Mandvi palace along with Rituraj. She had taken a break from her routine in Baroda and gone to the beach town on a supposed holiday. But she was here to help the poor locals. The fishermen and the people who continued with the traditional *Bhandani* cottage industry. Sitara didn't really understand the meaning of a holiday. She simply changed to a different mode of work or focussed on another set of people who had been marginalised by society. To her, that was enough of a break from routine.

As her personal assistant-cum-bodyguard, Rituraj never complained about Sitara's schedule which meant he worked all three hundred and sixty-five days of the year. As long as he could be with her, Rituraj had no issues.

"Welcome to the Gaekwad Palace, Prince Rajvardhan Thakore." Rituraj greeted the guest with folded hands.

"Thank you, Rituraj."

The ride to the palace took them barely five minutes and Rajvardhan was shown into a sitting room located to the right of the main hall of the palace. Taking in his opulent surroundings, Rajvardhan walked along with Rituraj and settled down in a corner of the long and low-slung sofa.

"Princess Sitara Devi should be with you in a minute," said Rituraj. "In the meanwhile, may I get you something to drink? Would you like some coffee or tea or maybe something stronger?"

"Coffee should be fine." Rajvardhan didn't think it was a good idea to drink along with the princess. Though he didn't know her personally, he had heard a bit about her before he got a whole dossier of information that Samrat had put together on her. Princess Sitara was a recluse who immersed herself in social work. She headed many charities and preferred to keep her work quiet.

He got up to greet her when she walked in just then. Tall and slim to a fault, the princess was clad in an ivory coloured, crepe silk sari, three ropes of translucent pearls decorating her slender neck. If he hadn't known for a fact that she was thirty-five, he would have thought that she was in her mid-twenties. Her face was unlined with minimal make-up while her hair was tied back in a low knot at the nape of her neck. Talk about understated elegance!

"Hello, Princess Sitara," he greeted once the secretary made the introductions.

She looked at him with piercing grey eyes as she responded, "Hello, Prince Rajvardhan, welcome to my home. Please sit down. Rituraj, have you sent for something? What would you like to have, Prince Rajvardhan?" Though soft, her voice was commanding.

A footman walked in just then with a heavily laden tray and placed it in front of Sitara. She sent him on his way with a flick of her wrist before pouring the fragrant coffee into two silver cups. Rituraj followed the footman, excusing himself.

She looked at her guest enquiringly before adding cream and sugar to both cups. She offered a cup and saucer to him along with a tiny silver spoon. "Here you go."

When they sat back to relish their coffee, Rajvardhan said, "I'm so glad that you could meet me at such short notice, Princess Sitara. And as I mentioned on the phone, the matter is urgent." He briefly told her about her ex-husband's engagement to Princess Chitrangada Vasudeva; how Gajanan had managed to trap her father into agreeing to the alliance. "It's like this, Princess Sitara. Harischandra Gajanan is a snake. It won't be enough just to return his money. He will not let go of Princess Chitrangada for just that. My intention is to create a strong enough case against the man. I'm…"

"Why are you telling me all this?" Sitara pinned her guest with her sharp gaze, without any expression on her face.

"Well, Princess Sitara, you used to be married to Raja Gajanan. That's why…"

She gave an incredulous laugh. "But that was, let me see, eighteen years ago. And I had been married to him for less than two years. What do you think I can do about the present situation?"

"If I've heard right, you do a lot of philanthropic work, don't you?" he asked, taking off at a tangent.

She gave him a regal nod. "So?"

"Couldn't you consider helping us with this one task where we hope an evil and cruel man finally ends up in jail? Chitrangada and I love each other and want to get married. It is simple enough for us to elope and get married. But," he paused and looked into her eyes, waiting for his words to sink in before continuing, "Gajanan is even capable of murdering her father. Simply returning his money isn't going to pacify him. He won't let Raja Bikram Vasudeva renege on his promise. I'm sure you understand." It was Rajvardhan's turn to pin her with his piercing brown gaze as he hadn't missed the way she winced on hearing the word 'murder'. He sat back on the sofa after pouring himself a second cup of coffee, relaxed about his approach to get under her skin. Now, he just had to wait for her to talk. He was confident that she would.

Sitara eyed the man in front of her and could see that he was being completely honest. Immediately after giving him an appointment, Rituraj had put together a dossier of information about Prince Rajvardhan Thakore for her to study. Not keen to read the entire file, she had run through the highlights typed out on a single sheet of paper. She had heard about the Thakores of Udaipur, of course. Reading through the sheet, she had realised that the family was as honest as they came. She sighed now, wishing, though uselessly, that she had had access to all information about her ex-husband, before they had tied the knot. But then, if that had been the case, her parents would have never got her married to Raja Harischandra Gajanan.

"Tell me, what do you want to know?"

"Thank you," said Rajvardhan. "You were married to Raja Gajanan for less than two years. May I ask you why you got divorced?"

She gave him a smile that didn't really reach her eyes. "I suppose that happened because of my lucky stars. To tell you the truth," she turned her gaze away to stare at the wall behind him sightlessly, "those twenty-two months were the worst period of my life. If I say that Harry is an animal, I would actually be insulting animals. He's a monster and a sadist.

He gets a kick out of others' pain." She uttered the words casually, in a dry and expressionless tone of voice. Her face remained passive and there was not even a slight flicker of emotion on it.

"Er… Princess…"

She raised a hand to stop him from talking. "Let me finish everything at one go." She looked at him then. "I hope what I am saying just stays with you." She continued when he nodded, "I needed many sittings of therapy to come out of the trauma that was my marriage. I was barely sixteen when I got married to him. My agenda was only to keep him happy. I accepted every kind of cruelty coming my way. He's the prototype of a sexual pervert." She had gone back to staring at the wall behind him. "Beating me up for the fun of it was an everyday incident. This continued for a year and a half and suddenly one fine day he wanted to find out why I wasn't getting pregnant. I don't really know what the doctor told him, but he stopped being violent and even tried to be nice to me in his own weird way." She shuddered at that point, but continued to speak in a steady voice, "After a couple of months, I was admitted to a maternity nursing home where a battery of tests was conducted on me." Her eyes moved forward to meet his as a soft laugh escaped her throat. "You know something, Harry thinks that everyone is an idiot and he's the only intelligent person on earth. He wasn't aware or bothered that I could read and write. The reports said clearly that there was nothing wrong with me. But he spread the word about me being barren. Harry assaulted the doctor who suggested that he should take some tests too. It would have been hilarious if it hadn't been pathetic. But then, didn't I say that my stars were lucky? That was my ticket to freedom, that I couldn't get pregnant with his child, due to no fault of mine."

"Did you go to the police? Didn't your parents have anything to say about it?"

"My parents were terribly upset. Till the time they passed on, they were sad that I was single and not happily married. They missed having grandchildren." She shuddered again. "Never again. Never will I let someone have that kind of power over me again. And to answer your question, we didn't go to the police. For one thing, Harry is pure evil and we didn't want him creating more trouble for us. For another, as I mentioned earlier, I had just had a lucky escape. Why would I go to the police?"

"But, Princess Sitara, isn't it only fair that the world knows what a blackguard Gajanan is? By keeping quiet, haven't you allowed him to go scot free and let him continue to harass other women? Do you know that Gajanan had married a second time?"

Princess Sitara gave a small nod, her mind working furiously. Was he right? Had she made a mistake in keeping quiet about her troublesome marriage? At the time of divorce, she had been completely shattered. So much so that it had taken her a very long time to realise that she was finally free of the demon she had been married to. The need to care for her had what had kept her parents going or they might have simply died of shock. None of them had really thought of making the information public. All said and done, it was not something one felt proud about and wanted to share with others.

"I heard about it."

"Did you know that his second wife was murdered?"

"What?" Sitara's eyes rounded in shock as she looked up at him, stunned. "Murdered? You mean Harry actually murdered his wife?" She shut her eyes, taking deep breaths to calm down her thundering heart, before opening them again. "That could have been me." Her voice was a soft whisper now.

"Precisely! That's exactly what I meant when I said that you should have exposed Gajanan for the monster he is."

"But how could I do that? Who would listen to me? He has so much power, such enormous clout over so many people. A number of politicians and policemen eat out of his hand. What sense would it make to go against him?"

Rajvardhan nodded. "You are right, Princess Sitara. I just need you to do one thing for us. You don't need to go public. I just want you to talk about your experience in front of a magistrate and it becomes part of the court record. This information will not be made public. It's only to get an arrest warrant against Gajanan."

"After all these years? Do you think it's possible?"

"With just your testimony, no. Your words will only form a part of the case I am putting together against Raja Gajanan. There will be much, much more. But, as someone who has suffered his cruelty, your statement will be of great help in helping other hapless women. I am there for Princess Chitrangada and she will escape. But there are bound to be other women who will continue to suffer at Gajanan's hands."

"You are right, Prince Rajvardhan. I never realised that my silence is probably the cause of many other women suffering at Harry's hands. That's so terrible, and I feel responsible for that woman's murder." There was remorse in Sitara's voice.

"I hope you won't beat yourself about it. You were only a teenager when you were divorced. And you had to pick up the pieces of your life. You…"

Sitara sighed. "Well, not directly responsible for her death. But… anyway, that's all water under the bridge. What should I do now? I will give my testimony against Harry most definitely."

"Thank you, Princess Sitara. That's truly nice of you. And I sincerely appreciate it." Rajvardhan got to his feet. "I'll take your leave now. Let me get an appointment and call Rituraj."

"Sure, Prince Rajvardhan. I'm glad to have the opportunity to make amends. Better late than never."

Rajvardhan took her leave, touched by her magnanimity. She was the injured party and she was talking about atonement. Princess Sitara was truly a great woman. He was all admiration for her.

Rituraj returned after dropping Prince Rajvardhan Thakore at the airport. "Is all well?" he asked Sitara.

She gave a deep sigh. "Is it, ever?" She briefly explained the reason for Rajvardhan's visit. "I have to go to the magistrate in Indore and give my statement. Will you make the arrangements?"

"Of course. Does next week work for you?"

She looked up into his eyes. What was with the spectacles? He had been sporting a pair since the last couple of years. She refused to believe that Rituraj needed one. Though she didn't ask him about it. "Why not? Our work should be done here. And Rituraj? I don't want to cross Harry's path," she said firmly.

"You won't, I promise," he said, equally firmly, a twinkle in his gaze. Harischandra wouldn't care for another beating from Rituraj, most definitely not. His royal reputation wouldn't withstand it for sure.

Sitara couldn't help smiling at him when she recalled the same incident.

13

Indore, 2002

Harischandra Gajanan found it a bit difficult to believe that his wife had quietly disappeared from his life. In his vanity and sheer idiocy, he had genuinely believed she would miss him terribly and would definitely try to get back with him. And what about her parents? Wouldn't Raja Manvendra Singh Gaekwad and Rani Vasundhara Devi want their daughter to get together with her estranged husband? But there was no news from the Gaekwad Palace.

His lawyer had advised Harischandra to set the ball rolling for the divorce proceedings only after the couple had lived separately for at least one whole year. It was barely three months and Harischandra was getting bored and restless. Gradually he had become obsessed with the idea of becoming a father. And how could he do that without a wife?

Should he simply bring Sitara back to the Gajanan Palace and reinstate her as his wife? She had after all cleared all the medical tests. Too impatient, Harischandra began to seriously consider it. But he had his pride. He definitely couldn't go to the Gaekwad Palace to reclaim his wife. That would be tantamount to admitting that he had been wrong all along.

A deep frown on his face, Harischandra paced the balcony outside his bedroom. Coming to a sudden decision, he went down to meet his father.

"Father, I have decided to bring Sitara back home," he declared baldly.

Raja Digvijay Gajanan looked up from his ornate desk where he had been writing something, a deep frown on his face. He was fed up of Harischandra and his tantrums by now and wasn't keen to support his son with his hare-brained schemes. He shrugged, saying, "You must do whatever makes you comfortable."

"Aren't you happy?" Harischandra snarled at his father, his teeth bared. Couldn't he ever please the old man?

Digvijay sighed, removing his glasses and keeping them on the table before rubbing his eyes. "You can't play with the girl's feelings like this, Harry. She's not a toy."

Harischandra stamped his foot, his temper suddenly spiralling out of control. "You disapprove of every damn thing I do. Go to hell!" He turned around and left his father's study, fuming. No, he didn't plan to say anything to his mother. She would also respond exactly like his father. He would send Hansraj, the oldest and most trustworthy servant in the palace, to go and bring Sitara back home. And maybe Rabri could go with him if the Gaekwads felt that their daughter needed a female escort.

"Hansraj, you leave immediately along with Rabri, go to Baroda and bring Princess Sitara home."

Hansraj looked at his young master, his face expressionless. All the servants in the palace were aware of the treatment Sitara had received at her spouse's hands. Rabri had been only too keen to spread the word. Now it looked like the *Yuvaraja* wanted his wife back. He couldn't help but feel sorry for the young Gaekwad princess. But then, it wasn't on his part to have an opinion, let alone express it. "*Ji Yuvaraja!*" he said, with folded hands.

The private plane left within the next two hours, the Rani insisting on sending a lot of sweets and other gifts to her daughter-in-law. Jhalkaribai missed Princess Sitara Devi terribly and felt deeply saddened by the way her son had abandoned the young woman.

The plane returned to Indore late at night and Harischandra was startled to find out that Hansraj and Rabri were back without Sitara.

Hansraj was trembling from head to foot, knowing fully well the *Yuvaraja* was capable of turning illogical and subsequently violent when he didn't get his own way. And it had fallen on his head to impart the news to Harischandra. Rabri had conveniently escaped to the kitchen, pleading urgent work. And Hansraj knew for a fact that she could get away with a lot as far as the prince was concerned.

"Why did you return without my wife?" Harischandra's voice was silky with menace as he looked at Hansraj with a grim expression on his face.

"*Yuvaraja,* the *Yuvarani* was not in the Baroda palace. She was travelling to…" Hansraj started stuttering as he wasn't used to fibbing. He deliberately didn't mention they hadn't even been allowed inside the gates of the palace. The message had been delivered to them through a palace guard who encouraged them to leave immediately. The guard's polite plea was nothing short of a threat.

"And where the hell has she gone?" Harischandra was beyond furious. Here he was, thinking of giving her a second chance. But it looked as if she had gone gallivanting. How dare she? He gnashed his teeth, glaring at the servant.

Hansraj bowed his head and kept mum. Anything he said could only land him in trouble at best or get him beaten in the worst-case scenario. He had found out Sitara Devi was in London, undergoing some kind of treatment. But he planned to share that information only with Rani Jhalkaribai and none other.

"Get out of my sight." Harischandra yelled at Hansraj who did an about turn and rushed out of the *Yuvaraja's* bedchamber, glad to have escaped unscathed.

It was Rabri who shared the information with Harischandra later in the night. "*Yuvaraja*," she said, a smile that bordered on a smirk languishing on her chubby face, "Your *Yuvarani* is in London. And you know something else? That tall, young man who was helping out at your wedding—Rituraj Srivastava—he has accompanied her." It was a rare occasion indeed when a female servant accompanied the *baraat* of a royal wedding. But then, Rabri was special to Harischandra. And right now, how she enjoyed adding fuel to the fire! Rabri grinned as she watched the temper explode on Harischandra's face. He hit her harder, making her glory in his violence as her orgasm was equally intense.

Harischandra climbed off Rabri and went to the bathroom, talking on the phone as he ordered his pilot to get the plane ready. He would deal with Hansraj after he returned from London, dragging home his errant wife by the hair.

Errant wife? But then logic and Harischandra weren't really the best of buddies.

He fretted and fumed while his pilot organised the requisite flight permits. As for a visa, Harischandra held a long-term visa to the UK because he travelled constantly and globally.

London, 2002

On landing at Heathrow, Harischandra went to the Gajanan mansion in Central London and freshened up as he waited for information from Bhaktavar, his personal assistant. The man was going to find out where Sitara was staying.

A couple of hours later, Harischandra rang the bell to the second-floor apartment in a private block in Mayfair, West End. His temper was flying high and he clenched his teeth. He was going to punch the daylights out of Sitara. How dare she hole up here with her lover boy? And that's what Rituraj must be, right? Harischandra was going to kick Rituraj's ass too. He vaguely remembered the lanky youth who had been running from pillar to post during the wedding ceremony. Beating up a slim, young man would be child's play and Harischandra looked forward to it with sadistic glee.

"Who is it?" It was a gruff male voice on the intercom.

"*Yuvaraja* Harischandra Gajanan," said he, in a pompous voice.

"Come on up," said the voice over the intercom before disconnecting.

Anger and excitement made Rituraj's blood zing as he felt a powerful adrenaline rush upon hearing Harischandra's voice on the intercom. He had never thought he would get an opportunity to punch the daylights out of this miserable scoundrel. And here he was being handed the chance on a platter. Pulling on his black leather boxing gloves with a maniacal grin on his face, Rituraj pressed the electronic code opening the door lock to let Sitara's husband enter their floor. Oh yes, she was still married to the rogue.

Harischandra heard a ping denoting the lock had opened. He pushed open the door and raced up the stairs, taking them two at a time, all set to throttle the man who had spoken to him so disrespectfully. How dare he order him to 'come on up' without even a greeting?

He imperiously knocked on the door located on the left of the staircase, that had a brass name plate reading, 'Gaekwad'. The door opened and before Harischandra could open his mouth to berate Sitara's illicit companion, a gloved fist landed on his face, hard. Literally speaking, Harischandra didn't know what hit him as he fell on his back on the marble floor, the side of his head hitting against the wall. He blacked out immediately.

Rituraj stood at the entrance, a wide grin on his malicious face as he looked down at the fallen *Yuvaraja*. Stepping out of the door, he kicked Harischandra who was currently sprawled on the floor of the foyer with a booted foot for good measure.

"Ritu, who's at the door?" Sitara walked into the living room as she spoke the words to Rituraj.

"Why don't you come and see for yourself?" he invited her over.

Sitara had been under treatment for two and a half months and was feeling more confident, mentally and physically. One more month and they would be returning home. She walked to the entrance and her jaw fell open when she saw Harischandra in this pathetic condition. "Have you killed him?" she asked Rituraj in a stunned whisper.

He laughed softly. "How I wish! But no. The bastard has fainted. Do you want me to wake him up with a bucket of water, maybe?"

It was Sitara's turn to grin. "Allow me," she said, walking back into the flat to open the fridge. "But what is he doing here?"

Rituraj shrugged. "I didn't wait to find out." He had just had enough time to pull on his boxing gloves after he heard Harischandra announce his name over the intercom.

Sitara brought back a bottle of chilled water from the fridge and walking over to her husband, poured the contents over his face. Maybe he would simply freeze to death!

But no such luck. Harischandra got up, sputtering, and shaking his head vigorously, a thin stream of blood running down from his nose. "What the fuck?!" He swore viciously, glaring at Sitara and Rituraj. "How dare you? How...?"

"I will dare even more if you don't leave immediately." Rituraj said firmly, his voice menacing and low. "You have chucked Princess Sitara Devi out of your life. How dare you come back to see her? Get out of her life and stay out!" he ordered the *Yuvaraja* of Indore.

Harischandra swore virulently, taking a threatening step towards Rituraj. "I'll kill you, you mother fucker. I…"

"You had better leave, Harry." Sitara didn't raise her voice when she spoke, looking Harischandra in the eye. She stood straight, appearing way healthier than the emaciated state she had been in when she left the Gajanan Palace with her father. She had never shown her fear to him, not during the twenty-two months she had lived in his palace as his wife. But it had been there, the dread, even if she had managed to push it deep inside the recesses of her mind. But now, after the many sessions with Dr. Gerard King, all the fears connected to her husband had been uprooted and she was free.

"I have decided to give you a second chance, Sitara."

"Second chance at what?" she asked, amazed at his gall. But then, Harischandra was never one to hesitate to do or say whatever he pleased. And it looked like it would please him to take her back as his wife.

"Being my princess and mother to my children, of course. What else?" He glared at her, running a hand over his nose which had swollen to double its size.

Sitara glanced at Harischandra as though he had crawled out from under a rock. "You are joking, right?"

"You think I've come all the way to London to joke with you, do you?" Harischandra's voice was a soft and menacing growl by now as he gave her a stern look. She looked more beautiful than before; her figure filled out in all the right places. Ugly temper blazed from his steely eyes suddenly. *Was it because of her affair with the man standing next to her? Stud*! Harischandra looked angrier than ever when he turned his gaze to Rituraj. Taller than the *Yuvaraja* by at least three inches, he was lean and muscular. Right now, his posture was menacing as well.

Sitara looked at her husband, disgust in her eyes. What had her parents seen in him that they had chosen Harischandra as her husband? But then, they weren't to know that he had an appallingly mean streak in him. Even now, they didn't know the full extent of the abuse she had suffered at his hands. But Dr. King was good. He had slowly weaned out the gory, lurid details from her. Almost everything! And the healing process was well underway. Dr. King was pleased with the changes in his patient. In fact, Sitara slept better nowadays. She smiled more. And Rituraj was such great company, always there for her, being a rock while asking for nothing in return.

She shook her head slowly at Harischandra, answering him, "I suppose you wouldn't."

Harischandra reached out a hand to take hers. "Let's go then. There's no need to pack anything. We…"

"Just a minute here." Rituraj went ahead to stand in front of Sitara, his stance threatening. "Sitara is going nowhere with you," he said firmly, his brown eyes spitting fire at the *Yuvaraja* of Indore.

"Who the hell are you to decide that? She's my wife and I'm taking her home to my palace." Harischandra stood toe-to-toe with Rituraj, his steely gaze clashing with the fire in Rituraj's gaze.

"I have been appointed by the Raja and Rani of Baroda to safeguard Princess Sitara Devi from harm, especially from a lowly *blackguard* such as you," said Rituraj, stressing the word 'blackguard', fully aware of how it would rankle with the other man. Since he couldn't find another reason to hit Harischandra, Rituraj had to be satisfied with calling him names.

"Are you sure you are doing only your job? And not something more than that?" Harischandra looked beyond Rituraj's shoulder to glare at Sitara. "Sitara, aren't you ashamed of hiding behind a man who's not your husband? Is something going on I should know about?" he asked spitefully.

Sitara stepped out from behind Rituraj and stood proudly straight in front of the monster who called himself her husband. "Whatever is between the two of us is none of your bloody business, Harry. It was you who chucked me out of your life. Allow me to sincerely thank you for it. Now get out of my life and stay out of it, do you hear? Or would you rather Rituraj beat the message into your head?" she asked, a shapely eyebrow raised in question, her gaze cold as she glared back at Harischandra.

More than making him angry, her demeanour aroused Harischandra, painfully. She appeared like a spirited lioness to him and he wanted badly to tap that passion in bed. Sitara had changed, grown up a lot in the few months she had been away from him and Harischandra realised he wanted his wife back desperately now. "You belong to me, Sitara!" he declared loudly, reaching out to take her hand in his, not seeing the fist come swinging at him once again before he was knocked out, a second time in the span of fifteen minutes.

This time, Harischandra wasn't lucky enough to black out. He lay on the floor, grimacing in pain as he reached out a hand to check his jaw. The crack had been loud when Sitara's bodyguard hit him. Surely, the mother fucker must have broken his jaw! The pain was excruciating, to say the least. Son of a bitch! He would get his back on that Rituraj bastard. He lay there on the marble floor, unable to get up even as he heard the door to the Gaekwad apartment shut.

I am going to kill the two of them with my bare hands!

The hooligans Harischandra hired to send after Rituraj were no match for the younger man's boxing skills. Over and above, Rituraj was a man on a committed mission, that of protecting Sitara from her husband. Finally, Harischandra knew that he was beaten and slunk way like the skunk he was, back to Indore where he could throw his weight about on those weaker than him.

15

There was a reason Rituraj began wearing spectacles at thirty. The glasses were as plain as they came. But he was sure that the thick black frame would be a deterrent to the women who felt the need to throw themselves at him. From the day he realised that he was in love with Sitara, he had never looked at another woman. But that still didn't stop them from finding him attractive.

Tall, dark and handsome, with intensely fiery brown eyes, Rituraj Srivastava was a sight to behold with his lean and well-honed physique only adding spice to his dashing looks. The one woman he liked— loved—didn't seem to want anything more than his friendship. Rituraj had quite easily worked his way into Sitara's life in such a manner that she would need him for everything. Only the royal princess appeared to take it for granted. Not that it really mattered to her Man Friday as long as he got to spend all his waking hours with her.

Single women from the age of seventeen to forty seemed to lust after him. Ugh! Couldn't they understand a straightforward and terse refusal? In his mind's eye, Rituraj perceived himself to be a nerd.

He liked his books, he was passionate about boxing, he watched films, taking an interest in them only after Harshvardhan took up acting as a career, and he slogged on a daily basis to make Sitara's professional life as smooth as possible. Over the years, the princess had set up many charity trusts, helping people from the lower income group, in Baroda to begin with. Later, she had spread her wings all over Gujarat and also in other parts of India. Rituraj managed her appointments, her trips around the country, her accounts and anything else which required to be done.

He had turned the adage, 'Behind every successful man is a woman', on its head. It was Rituraj behind Sitara's success, all the way. And it didn't really matter to him if she was aware of it. His love for her was unconditional and he was ready to lay down his life for her.

One fine day, fed up with the excessive attention he was getting from yet another woman he was coordinating with on Sitara's behalf, Rituraj decided to do something about it. He got himself a pair of plain glasses with a thick and large black frame. Looking in the mirror, he decided that nobody would notice him now, completely unaware of his own charisma. The photochromatic lens turned smoky in sunlight and made him look smoking hot.

"Good morning Rituraj. You are wearing glasses." Sitara stated the obvious before asking, "How come?" when he walked into the library on the day he had acquired them.

Rituraj shrugged his wide shoulders, giving her a gentle smile. She looked gorgeous sitting in the sunshine lighting up the room through the east-facing windows, her face glowing with good health, her golden skin enhanced by the turquoise coloured sari that she wore. "Good morning, Sitara. They are for reading." Which was so not true. "I had them made in such a way that I could wear them all the time since pulling them on and off my nose will prove to be a task," he grinned charmingly at her.

Sitara's heart gave a leap as she looked up at his roguish grin. If anything, the spectacles made him look better than before. She gave a soft sigh, pushing back the regrets within herself. It was sad they could never belong together. After all, she had been married once. How could she tarnish Rituraj's life by thrusting herself into it? And then there was the matter of her ex-husband. Harischandra was truly a dog in the manger. She didn't want Rituraj to suffer at the horrid Harischandra's hands. Once had been more than enough.

She smiled at him now. "I know what you mean. Looks good. Let's get breakfast before attacking those mails, shall we?" she said, pointing to her in-tray that was as usual piled up with envelopes.

"Sure, let's go," he said, giving her a nod. Well, he couldn't very well tell her that he would rather have her for breakfast, could he?

And Rituraj continued to ward off the women who threw themselves at him during the course of his work.

Sitara couldn't help noticing the way Rituraj attracted women's attention, like honey to bees. In the beginning, she was amused and even teased him regarding it. He was her friend, and she was comfortable pulling his leg. She didn't realise how frustrating he found the experience as it seemed as if she herself wasn't in the least aware of him as a stunning specimen of manhood. But that was before the one-time Sitara had become completely and one hundred per cent aware of Rituraj.

How she wished she could wipe away those few days from her life! And maybe his too!

16

Baroda, 2005

Almost four years had rolled by since Sitara returned home from Indore and two years since her divorce had been finalised. She had gone back to university after returning from London and her treatment with the psychiatrist. Her confidence regained, Sitara had chosen to get a degree in Social Work and Human Resource Management from the MS University in Baroda.

But the Raja and Rani still couldn't swallow the fact that their young daughter, the apple of their eye, getting thrown out of her home by her husband and later getting divorced. Manvendra Singh Gaekwad took to bed soon after Sitara's divorce. While he completely sided with his daughter and had accepted her back into his royal household with open arms, it still didn't mean he could digest the turn her life had taken. Patriarchal to the core, he couldn't help worrying about her future. What would she do? Who would take care of her after his demise? Harshvardhan was a teenager and exceptionally attached to his sister. But there would come a time when he would want to move on with his life. Who would take care of Sitara then? Sitara needed to be taken care of was a thought which was firmly entrenched in her father's mind.

Rituraj's face flashed before his mind's eye. The boy was loyal to the royal family and had proved himself again and again. He had been like a rock, taking care of Sitara during her stay in London. The Raja, while not knowing the exact details, was well aware of Harischandra's visit to London and how Rituraj had protected Sitara from any emotional setback during that crucial phase. He sent for Rituraj now.

The young man walked into the Raja's room, looking like a warrior. Manvendra Singh smiled. It looked as if living in the palace amidst royalty had rubbed off on his ex-accountant's son.

"Come here, my boy. Pull that chair closer and sit next to me."

"*Ji, Rajaji,*" said Rituraj respectfully, doing as the Raja instructed.

Manvendra Singh took Rituraj's hand in his and looked at his face with eyes shimmering with unshed tears. "Rituraj, listen. After I pass on…"

"Please, *Rajaji,* don't talk like that." Rituraj reached out to enclose the Raja's wrinkled left hand in both of his strong ones. "You will lead a long life. You have to, for our sakes."

The Raja shook his head from left to right, some strange instinct driving him on. "Listen to me. May I ask you for a favour?"

Rituraj felt tearful as he looked at the tired face in front of him. Manvendra Singh was just fifty-two years old. But he looked so old now. His sickness had eaten into him. Dr. Kanjilal said that it was a stomach bug. In all probability anguish and despair at what his daughter had suffered had eaten into his soul. He said, "*Hukum kijiye, Rajaji.*"

"Will you be there for my Sitara, always?" The Raja lifted his trembling right hand, palm facing upwards. "I will not ask you to wed her, only because she's already been married and shunned by her husband and not because you aren't a royal yourself. How I wish…" He took a deep breath to stabilise his failing vocal cords before continuing, "How I wish I had got her married to you, Rituraj, instead of that devil Gajanan." Tears ran unashamedly down both sides of the Raja's face, wetting the pillow.

Rituraj wanted to cry himself. At twenty-three, he had never looked at another woman. It was not really necessary to actually marry the woman he loved. He knew for a fact that he belonged to her until death claimed one of them. "Now that you have spoken your mind, *Rajaji*, I will marry Sitara Devi if she will have me for her husband. And that's a promise. As for taking care of her, you may shed your worries right now. I will be her shadow, forever."

The Raja gave him a weak smile, his eyes brightening a little on hearing Rituraj's words. The worry crushing his heart seemed to have reduced a little. "Go now. And ask Vasundhara to see me."

It took about a month of careful nursing before the Raja was on his feet. Rituraj's promise to take care of Sitara had brought hope to Manvendra Singh and Vasundhara Devi.

One evening, during his visit to check on the Raja, Dr. Kanjilal Trivedi suggested, "Why don't you and the Rani take a holiday from your palace duties? It will do both of you a world of good."

Manvendra Singh turned to look at his wife. "What do you say, Vasundhara?"

"Are you sure the Raja is fit enough to travel, doctor?" asked Vasundhara, appearing tired.

"Don't go too far. Just a short trip somewhere nearby, ideally to a seashore."

Vasundhara brightened up, turning and addressing her husband, "Why don't we go to Mandvi? It's been a while."

Manvendra Singh nodded, feeling enthusiastic. Their palace in Mandvi would make for a relaxing vacation. "Why not?"

They decided to leave in three days on a private plane specially hired for the trip.

They left on Friday morning, waving 'goodbye' to both Sitara and Rituraj who had both gone to the aerodrome to see them off, looking forward to spending a month at the Mandvi Palace.

The Raja and Rani never reached their destination as their plane exploded in mid-air. Even their broken bodies were located a slight distance away from the crash.

That the royal siblings and Rituraj were heartbroken was putting it mildly. Harshvardhan rushed back from Los Angeles where he was currently studying.

It fell on Rituraj's shoulders to take responsibility as both the prince and the princess were far too dazed at both their parents dying in the unexpected accident. He managed the funerals and dealt with all the people who visited the palace to offer their condolences. Relatives thronged the palace, shocked by the sudden deaths of both the Raja and Rani of Gaekwad.

Sitara and Harshvardhan bore their grief bravely, presenting a courageous front while completely shattered from within. Only Rituraj was privy to what the royal prince and princess actually felt.

Royals or not, they had been a close-knit family. The brother-sister duo was traumatised by their parents' death. And both of them were well aware that Rituraj was equally upset since he had looked upon the Raja and Rani as his parents after his own passed away.

The Gaekwad Palace was completely bogged down with grief. After fifteen days, it was time for Harshvardhan to go back to his studies in the USA.

Harshvardhan hugged Sitara tightly as he took leave of her. Pressing his lips to her forehead, he said, "You take care, Sitara *di*." His deep grey eyes were wet with unshed tears as he patted her cheek. "I'll see you during my Christmas break. Why don't you come over, *di*? It'll be a good change for you too." He looked at her hopefully, having thought of it that very moment.

Sitara smiled at her younger brother through her tears. How tall he had grown during the year he had been living abroad! "Not just now, Harsh. I haven't done much work over the last few weeks. There are some urgent matters pending which need to be taken care of. You go on and study well. And take care of yourself, okay?"

Harshvardhan nodded. "But don't forget to make a plan, will you?" He turned to Rituraj and said, "Will you bring Sitara *di* over to Los Angeles? Please?"

Rituraj gave Harshvardhan a sad smile, saying, "Of course I will, Harsh, if Sitara wants to go."

"You're getting late, Harsh. Don't worry about me. I will make a plan soon," said Sitara in a half-promise. Right now, she wanted to simply lock herself in her room and howl her heart out. She felt so alone in the world.

Harshvardhan left, waving 'goodbye' to both of them. He had refused Rituraj's offer to go to the airport with him. "No, Rituraj. You please stay back with Sitara *di*. She needs you now more than ever."

Did she? Rituraj wasn't so sure.

A few days before they left on their fatal trip, Rani Vasundhara Devi called Rituraj aside and spoke with him regarding the promise he had made to the Raja.

"Listen, Rituraj. Do you think of me as your mother?" she asked in a gentle voice, an emotional smile on her face.

"But of course, Rani *ma*. Do you even need to ask?" Rituraj said immediately, feeling equally emotional. After all, hadn't the Raja and Rani been like parents to him after his own died?

Vasundhara Devi held his lean cheeks in her hands, and stared at him adoringly. "You could have been my own child in another lifetime. I am sure of it. I am genuinely worried about Sitara, Rituraj. She's barely twenty-two and has no one. Harsh will grow up and make a life of his own. But…" she paused, wondering how to broach the subject, but only for a few seconds. Clearing her throat, Vasundhara Devi continued to speak, "I know you promised the *Rajasahib*, to marry Sitara. I feel quite certain you love Sitara, don't you?" she asked.

Rituraj gave her a small smile, nodding his head. "You think right, Rani *ma*."

"It's just that, Rituraj, just because…" she paused yet again, looking at his dear face before continuing in a rush, "Let me tell you straight. I know you are an affectionate and loyal boy. But I don't want you to feel as if you owe it to the Raja and me to marry Sitara. Do you see what I mean? She's already been married once and divorced. I…"

Rituraj lifted a hand and placed it over the Rani's mouth, effectively stopping her from speaking further. Shaking his head, he said, "I don't care about that, Rani *ma*. And there's no question of feeling obliged. I'll marry Sitara if she'll have me." He laughed softly, feeling a sense of joy creeping into his heart. It was wonderful to know that Sitara's parents wanted him as their son-in-law as much as he desired Sitara.

But the saddest part was the Raja and Rani had planned to raise the topic with Sitara once they returned from their holiday.

What about Sitara herself? Had she ever considered getting married again? Was it possible her affection for him was sincere but platonic? He sighed. It was not the right time to broach the subject anyway.

Moreover, while in London, Sitara had sworn she would never marry again, not ever. Rituraj sighed, and mentally shrugged off the thoughts of 'happily ever after'. He had no agenda other than Sitara. And he was an extremely patient person. He was there for her to lean on, be it as a friend, a husband or even as her Man Friday.

17

Baroda, 2005

Sitara somehow managed to control her sorrow over the next few days after Harshvardhan left. But she simply broke down one evening immediately after dinner as she sat in the library on her father's chair.

When Rituraj went into the library to exchange his book, he was startled to hear her soft hiccups. He turned direction, dropping the book he was carrying on to a chair as he walked swiftly towards her. "Sitara!"

Sitara didn't lift her face which was buried in her arms on the desk, her body shaking with grief as she sobbed in a completely unrestrained manner.

"Sitara, sweetheart!" Unable to bear her pain, Rituraj placed his hands on her quivering shoulders, wondering how to console her.

Sitara lifted her head to look at the compassion on his face and broke down once again. "Ritu!" she groaned, turning about to throw her arms around his lean waist and bury her face in his flat stomach, crying all the more.

Rituraj held her close, his heart beating heavily as he tried his best to absorb her suffering, one arm around her shoulders as he pulled her close to his body, while the other hand stroked her head gently. Rituraj deliberately kept his touch platonic and he made soothing noises, exactly the way one would deal with an injured pup or a kitten. He didn't say anything, afraid of what might come out of his mouth, having just realised he had called her 'sweetheart'.

It was a long while before Sitara calmed down, warm and cosy as she snuggled close to his huge body, feeling secure by the gentle stroking on her head. How she wished she could remain where she was, forever! But no! How could she? Rituraj was too nice a person to be saddled with someone like her! Someone who had been married to the devil for almost two years; someone who had been dragged down to the depths of debauchery. Some might argue that she had been an unwilling participant, but then she had been a party to it.

Sitara got up suddenly, feeling restless, her body tightening with an unfamiliar need now that her grief was spent. Only, Rituraj was standing too close and she literally fell into his arms.

"Ritu!" Sitara's voice was a whisper as she looked up into his blazing dark eyes, her own gaze a highly turbulent cloudy grey.

"Sweetheart!" He couldn't help calling her that. How could he not when he was burning with desire for her? Not just to offer solace, but also to… also to… what? Rituraj took a deep breath before he admitted to himself, *Yes, I want to make love to her*.

Red bloomed on Sitara's cheeks when she noticed, not just the endearment, but the tenderness in his voice as he uttered the word. "Ritu!" She seemed to have lost control of her body and mind as she lifted her face to press her lips to his cheek, her tongue peeping out to stroke against the roughness, a deep sigh emanating from her as she revelled in the texture.

Rituraj's arms involuntarily tightened around Sitara's waist, his fingers splayed on the bared waist between the drape of her sari and blouse. He inadvertently crushed her to his broad and muscular chest, delighting in her softness.

Sitara buried her face in the crook of his shoulder, breathing deeply as she took in his clean masculine scent. He must have had a shower after dinner. He smelled of pine-scented soap and something else she couldn't quite put a finger on… something unique to Rituraj. She opened her eyes a slit and was startled to see her left hand on his right shoulder, tracing the contours slowly and deliciously. *What has come over me? What am I doing?* But she couldn't stop herself as she watched her hand caress his chest, her palm rubbing against a flat male nipple which swiftly perked up at her attention, pressing against her hand through his shirt. Her attention shifted to the crisp hair that tingled her palm, making her want to rip his clothing off.

Sitara lifted shocked eyes up to his face, suddenly afraid of herself and was shaken when she caught the burst of passion in his fiery brown eyes. "Ritu…"

"I want you, Sitara." There! He had put it into words, his need for her. No, he wasn't yet ready to declare his love. That would depend on what she felt for him. Right now, Rituraj could see she was lonely and needed him with a kind of desperation. But he wasn't sure if it was him she needed or anyone would have done in this situation. Yes, put that way, it did sound rather callous, but he was only trying to be honest here. Sitara was so young and had lived a battered life in a short span of two decades. Her parents' deaths on top of all that, just when she had recovered and was trying to build a life for herself, was truly a cruel twist of fate. Just now, he was there for her, giving her solace. But not at the cost of declaring his love. Unless he was sure that it was, or would be, reciprocated.

Sitara threw her arms around Rituraj's neck and locked her hands behind his head, pressing her lips to the corner of his mouth. "Please make love to me, Ritu," she said in a passionate whisper.

Are you sure? No, Rituraj didn't say the words out loudly. But he wasn't one to look at a gift horse in the mouth. And well, his intentions were honourable enough and he did have the blessings of both the Raja and Rani of Gaekwad, to woo and wed their daughter. With a mental shrug, Rituraj turned his head to press his lips to hers. "You'll have to show me how."

Sitara jumped back, as if burnt. "What???" she asked, her gaze disturbed. Did he mean what she thought he meant? Was Rituraj inexperienced at making love? Did that mean he was a... virgin? She blanched. This was something Sitara simply hadn't anticipated. Okay, to be truthful, she had never really thought about it. Sitara stared at him, a confused look in her eyes now.

Rituraj gave her a weak smile, his arms feeling empty as they lay against his sides, his body taut with need. He gave her a small nod. "You understood me."

"Are you a virgin?" Sitara asked him in a hoarse whisper. He was twenty-three, dammit!

He grimaced. "Guilty."

"Why? I mean, how come?" She stared at him, trying to make some sense of what he said. He looked so handsome and she was sure there had been no dearth of opportunities. She had noticed women, both young and old, staring at him, whenever they were outside the palace; even in London. She had felt the burgeoning desire in his taut body as it was thrust against hers a short while ago. He was obviously heterosexual. Then why? Not waiting for his reply, she turned away, walked to the window and stared out sightlessly at the garden. She now felt rather stupid, propositioning him. Also, the whole episode somehow created an awkward vibe between them.

Rituraj scowled. Why did it matter that he was a virgin? The fact was that he had discovered he was in love with a married woman when he was barely seventeen. After that, he had never wanted to make love with anyone else. He was particular like that, wanting to give himself only to the woman he loved. At that point, he hadn't held much hope of ever making love to any woman, not in this lifetime. But it looked like destiny had a different plan for him, way better than what he had imagined.

"Sitara…" Rituraj followed her to the window, his footsteps hushed as he walked across the thick carpet, placing gentle hands on her shoulders. "Does it matter?" He pressed his body to hers, his throbbing manhood twitching against her curved bottom. "I know you want me too." He turned her around to hold her close to his chest, kissing the top of her head. Placing his fingers under her chin, he lifted her face to his. "You are experienced. Won't you teach me? Show me how?"

Blood rushed into Sitara's face as she looked deeply into his eyes burning with desire. Was she the right person for it? He wasn't aware of the debauchery she had suffered at Harischandra's hands. Did she know how to *make love* in the normal sense? Did she even know what normal lovemaking was? Sitara shuddered. But then, didn't that make her a virgin as well? Not physically, maybe, but mentally, most definitely, as she had never experienced the joys of making love, but only the pain of perverted sex.

The desire fizzled out of Rituraj's gaze as it clouded with disappointment at her continued silence. He removed his arms from around her and walked back a few steps, a deep sigh shuddering through him. "I understand," he said, not really meaning it. Dammit all to hell! Why did he have to love the princess of Gaekwad? To the exclusion of all other women? He walked swiftly towards the door, determined to get to the private gym in the basement of the palace which used to serve as a dungeon in yonder days. He needed his punching bag more than anything else in the world right now.

"Ritu!" Sitara called out in a commanding voice, following him swiftly. She placed a hand on his forearm, gripping the tense muscle as she asked, "What did you understand?" a tremor in her voice.

Refusing to look at her even as he stopped in his tracks, Rituraj said, "I understand that you don't want to make love with me."

Sitara laughed, unable to stop the rush of mirth gurgling from her throat. She leaned her face against his arm, tucking her hand in his elbow. "Don't be an idiot, Ritu. Want to see how hard my heart is beating for you?" She took his other hand and placed it against the left side of her chest, applying pressure as she looked deeply into his eyes, her laughter disappearing even as her body reacted to his touch.

"Sitara…" Rituraj shut his eyes, his dark and thick eyelashes resting against his lean and masculine cheeks even as deep colour ran up his face, all his senses tuned into the softness of her breast as his hand lay above her heart which seemed to beat in unison with his own prancing one. His hand curled around the left breast, squeezing it gently, revelling in its plumpness.

Sitara pressed her body closer, encouraging him, loving the feel of his gentle touch on her clamouring body. "Ritu…" There was hunger in her voice and gaze as she looked up at him before kissing him on his mouth, drawing a damp tongue over the seam of his masculine lips, rejoicing in the texture.

"Sss…" Rituraj pulled her close to his body which had gone hard with desire, caressing her back with his left hand. He groaned when Sitara bit his lower lip, opening his mouth inadvertently to let her in, not sure what hit him when he was bombarded with sensations as he felt her tongue tangle with his.

When Rituraj didn't open his mouth while she traced her tongue over his lips, Sitara bit his lip, hoping to get entry into his mouth. She got what she wanted when Rituraj groaned, smiling to herself as she pushed her tongue into his warm mouth, running the tip over his teeth before encountering his tongue and tangling with it. Time stood still as they explored each other's mouths, coming up for air from time to time. Kissing Rituraj was so different from… no, she wasn't going to take the devil's name; not at this time, if at all ever. She pressed closer to Rituraj, wanting more.

Rituraj lifted his face to look down at the woman in his arms, a smile on his face as he noticed the high colour riding on her soft cheeks. Sitara looked beyond beautiful! Following his instincts, he buried his face in the crook of her neck, his mouth seeking the heavily beating pulse there as he rubbed his tongue over the erroneous zone back and forth, thrilled to find it racing all the faster. He nuzzled her cheek, taking deep breaths as he drew in her perfume, a combination of sandal and incense, all woman at that. He pressed open mouthed kisses along her jawline before reaching her right ear, the tip of his tongue touching her lobe.

Sitara moaned with longing as his kisses roused long-dormant emotions, tilting her head to encourage his foraging mouth, hanging on to his muscular shoulders for dear life. If she hadn't had her arms around his neck, she would have simply slid to the floor as her rubbery legs wouldn't have been able to hold her up. She moaned all the louder when he nipped her lobe with his teeth. "Ritu…"

Realising that he was on the right track, Rituraj traced the whorl of her ear with his tongue before blowing gently into it, smiling when he heard her groan yet again. "You like?" he asked in a whisper right into her ear.

Sitara gave a nod, saying, "Too much."

He laughed softly, lifting her up in his arms and carrying her to a low-slung couch which was big enough to accommodate the two of them, before laying her down on it. Looking down at himself, he laughed some more when he noticed that all the buttons of his shirt had been pulled open.

Sitara blushed fierily, staring up at Rituraj as he shrugged out of his shirt, his magnificent shoulders coming into view. By God! He looked too handsome for words. And what a wonderfully sculpted body he had! She almost drooled at the sight, even as her gaze travelled down his broad chest to his washboard abs before stopping at the line of dark and crisp hair arrowing down below his navel. She swiftly lifted her gaze to look into his eyes, a shapely eyebrow up in query. "Do you need my help in taking off the rest of your clothes?" she asked saucily, a small grin on her face.

Refusing to admit to the awkwardness inundating him, Rituraj crossed his arms over his chest and raised his left brow at her, his gaze running over her delicious body encased in a simple cotton sari. The sari *pallu* had fallen off her shoulder to expose her luscious breasts encased in a figure-hugging blouse, making him grow even harder than before. She looked simply gorgeous, her lips red from the passionate kisses they had shared just now. "I suppose we can help each other," he said, kneeling down beside her, placing a caressing hand over her bare stomach. "Tell me! Where do I start?" he asked, innocence and desire warring with each other in his melting chocolate eyes.

Sitara got up as if in a trance, her equally tumultuous gaze locked with his, taking his hand to place it at the front of her blouse. "Help me, Ritu."

Rituraj gulped before bringing forth his other hand to open the hooks that held the front of her blouse together, his hands trembling as they went about their task.

Sitara looked down at his large hands, the fingers long with neatly maintained nails—an absolute turn on indeed—with a soft smile on her face even as colour bloomed in her cheeks. This huge giant, her bodyguard, was truly a softie. She held his manly wrists as he finished removing all the hooks before parting the flaps of the blouse, his eyes devouring her lace-encased breasts. She felt her body respond with alacrity, the tips of her breasts perking up and nudging against the lace. She was enthralled by his fascinated gaze running over her upper body, feeling all woman and a highly desirable one at that.

Rituraj placed his hands on her breasts, squeezing them gently at first and applying pressure when he felt her eager response. "You have a beautiful body," he said in a voice gone hoarse even as he ran his tongue over lips gone dry.

"So do you," she responded, placing her hands on his wide shoulders and running them down his muscular arms, loving the feel of steel encased in velvet.

Rituraj tried to remove the blouse off Sitara without much success as her hands were on his body. He gave up too soon, caught up in the maelstrom of sensations created by Sitara's soft hands running over his upper body. He pulled her closer to his chest, revelling in the feel of her hands running over his naked back from shoulder to waist.

Sitara sighed softly, her eyes studying his face as she caressed his back, his skin smooth and tight to the touch. "Kiss me," she commanded, eyeing his parted lips hungrily.

He bent his head to press his mouth to hers, his breath leaving him in a whoosh as she opened her mouth and drew his tongue within, sucking on it ravenously. When they came up for air, it was Rituraj's turn to demand, "Help me take your clothes off, Sitara. I want to see you."

She gave him a sultry smile before taking her hands off his body to pull her blouse off swiftly. She twisted around to show him her back, saying, "Will you remove the hook?"

Rituraj followed her instruction by removing the single hook that held her bra in place. Pushing the straps off her shoulders, his hands reached out in the front to cup her bare breasts in his hands, his palms pressing against the tips as he squeezed them.

Sitara pressed her naked back to his chest, rubbing against the crisp hair, loving the contrast in their body textures, her hands pressed over his as they pleasured her breasts. She lifted her arms to lock them around his neck, pulling his head towards hers as she turned her own to kiss him.

Rituraj drew infinite pleasure as he petted her firm breasts, tweaking the nipples with his thumbs and forefingers when he heard her loud moan. He stopped what he was doing to ask her, "Did I hurt you?"

Sitara shook her head, her hair which had fallen out of the loose knot it had been held in, now splayed all over his chest. "Not at all. Please don't stop."

He smiled, turning her around to face him before bending down to kiss the valley between her breasts, his lips exploring the curves as he turned to the left and then to the right as he pressed kisses all over her chest.

"Will you take me in your mouth, Ritu?" she asked, her voice pleading, the turgid tips of her breasts begging for his caresses.

He lifted his head to look at her face as he continued to kneel next to the couch, trying to grasp her request. Reaching forward, he drew a damp tongue around an aureole, making her gasp in rapture.

Sitara placed her hands on his head, pulling his face closer to her body and shut her eyes with a sigh when his lips closed over a taut nipple. "Ritu..." She ran her hands over his hair which was the texture of raw silk, her fingers running through it repeatedly in a caress.

Encouraged by her sighs and moans, Rituraj sucked deeply on her breast, loving the soft texture, his hands stroking her waist.

Sitara gently moved her body, encouraging him to make love to her other breast, taking his hand and placing it over it.

Rituraj followed her lead, turning his head to kiss her right breast, his hand closing over her left, his palm brushing over the damp and swollen tip, swamped by the myriad sensations.

It was a long while before Sitara got up, indicating that he should also stand up. She stood in front of him, her breasts thrust forward proudly, revelling in her femininity. For the first time since she was married, she felt like an equal partner. Giving him a smile, she reached out to the buckle on his belt, removing it before unzipping his pants.

"Let me." Rituraj stepped out of his pants, leaving his briefs on, reaching out to pull her sari out of her petticoat.

Sitara removed the knot which was holding her petticoat in place, kicking both the garments away before standing in front of him wearing only a minuscule pair of pastel pink panties, her arms at her sides as she looked deeply into his eyes. "I want you inside me, Ritu."

He nodded, reaching out to pull her panties down her long, slim legs.

Sitara reached out to hang on to his shoulder, lifting her legs one by one as he pulled the panties completely off her. "Now it's your turn," she said, helping him out of his briefs, her eyes studying his manhood greedily as it grew longer and harder right in front of her eyes. She ran a hand down the length of his penis, curling it around him, laughing softly when she heard him groan. "You feel so good."

Rituraj copied her gesture as he placed his hand on her triangular mound, caressing it, his touch a tad rough.

Sitara widened her legs, encouraging him to use his fingers as he slid one inside her vagina, exploring her depths. She pressed closer to his caressing hand, turning her head to kiss his chest, running her tongue over a flat male nipple. Moaning when he increased the pressure by adding one more finger as he caressed her, she bit his nipple, making him grunt in response.

Removing his fingers from within her, Rituraj pulled her close to his body before lifting her yet again to lay her down on the couch, joining her this time. He rose above her, studying her flushed body with greedy eyes even as he felt her guide his manhood inside her. He groaned as he slid into her smoothly, her body wet and inviting, opening up to him completely. He settled in with another grunt before instinctively lifting himself out before thrusting again.

Just as the pleasure built up, it was all over even before it began, Rituraj coming almost immediately with a loud groan. He fell on top of her, completely spent at the unexpected orgasm which arrived way too soon, burying his face against her neck.

Sitara was confused for just a moment before a soft smile lit her features, her arms going around him. It was his first time, after all! It was a wonder he had lasted this long. She hugged him close, kneading his back caressingly. If she knew what she was doing, it wouldn't be long before he was ready for an encore.

Rituraj sighed. He supposed it had been pleasurable, to an extent. But it had been too quick, not giving him, or her for that matter, much time for a build-up. Sure that Sitara must be disappointed at his not-so-good performance; he tried to move away from her, only to find her tightening her arms around him. He was surprised by the strength she displayed as her slender arms hugged him close to her body, refusing to let him go.

He lifted his head to look down at her. "Sitara… I'm sorry. I…" He didn't have a choice but to stop talking when she placed a hand over his mouth, shaking her head from side to side.

"Don't be, Ritu. It was your first time and I think you were just way too aroused…"

He smiled, relaxing, kissing the hand which lay across his mouth. "Oh, that I was. Actually, it looks like I'm getting excited once more."

Sitara laughed softly when she felt him stirring against her thigh, her throat choking up when he bit the pad of her thumb, her eyes glowing with rekindled desire. "I can see that you are," she said in a hoarse voice even as she reached out to touch his growing erection, caressing him from the root to the tip, smiling when she felt him growing harder yet.

"I don't want to fail you this time," he said, a determined tilt to his square chin as he ran his hand over her left breast.

"You have never failed me, Ritu, not ever," she declared passionately, reaching out to kiss him on his mouth. He had been her champion right from the beginning. Why the hell had her parents not thought of marrying her off to Rituraj? Sitara couldn't help that marvellous thought from springing to her mind. Life would have been so much more beautiful and happier. *But then*, she sighed, *honi ko kaun taal sakta hai*? What was meant to happen would have happened eventually.

Her sigh turned to an impassioned moan when she felt Rituraj's mouth closing over the tip of her breast, wet pooling between her thighs as he sucked gently at first and then hard. "You keep that up and I promise you that you can't fail this round. I'm all eager and wet for you, Ritu," she whispered deliciously into his ear before nipping at the lobe.

Rituraj reached out a finger to verify for himself as he dipped it into her vulva. Oh yes, she had been speaking the truth. He lifted himself above her, drawing her left leg around his waist before plunging into her depths, grunting with satisfaction when she closed around him like a velvet glove. He rode her hard, his lips seeking her mouth as he thrust his tongue into it rhythmically, matching the rhythm of his tumescent manhood plunging into her. His hands stroked her breasts, gently pinching the tips, making her sigh with pleasure.

Sitara felt the orgasm building from deep down her womb as her nails dug into his smooth back, completely unaware of the marks she was leaving on him. Her body thrashed on the couch as she sought out for something that was just out of reach, clinging to Rituraj as sweat ran off her forehead in small rivulets to disappear into her hair.

"Sitara, my sweetheart," Rituraj groaned, desperately trying to control the orgasm that was all set to burst from within him. No, he had to let her find pleasure first. With a determined thrust of his chin, he bent down to kiss her breast, suckling deeply.

That's when it happened! The earth shattered all around her as Sitara came, as she had never come before. None of Harischandra's, or Rabri's ministrations for that matter, had made Sitara reach the peak of pleasure. Nowhere near as what she was feeling now. She felt as if her body had been ripped apart with her soul floating somewhere out there in the universe before it all came together to become one whole again. Yes, only for a couple of minutes, but she felt as if she had been reborn.

Rituraj groaned long and loud as he felt her come apart in his arms before he exploded in a climax which humbled him, almost bringing him to his knees. He didn't know that tears were pouring down his face, not before he felt Sitara gently wiping them away as she hugged him close.

18

Rabri watched in fascination as Harischandra paced furiously up and down the Gajanan Palace terrace, his black temper pervading the atmosphere as it seemed to gush forth from every pore of his body. She turned her head to look over the parapet wall, her heart thumping in anticipation as she noticed the broken flower pots that he had thrown over the rocks, the plants themselves having tumbled out along with the soil and lying strewn around, appearing forlorn. There was a reason for her excitement. They had the best sex when Harischandra was in a rage and she couldn't wait for him to return to her.

The *Yuvaraja* turned around to look at the palace maid, as if on cue, his eyes glittering menacingly. "Come here!" he ordered in a guttural voice, crooking a forefinger at her.

Rabri walked forward eagerly only to be grabbed none-too-gently by Harischandra. He placed a hand at her waist to tear away her sari and petticoat before thrusting himself into her as he took her right there against the wall. She moaned deliriously, having been ready and waiting for this from the moment she walked up to the terrace in his wake.

Harischandra had been in a fuming temper from the time he had returned from London, his nose broken and his jaw swollen. Rabri wasn't a fool to ask him what had happened. But she had formed her own ideas regarding the same. Being shrewd, she had kept her eyes and ears open when she went to the Gaekwad Palace along with old Hansraj to bring Harischandra's wife back to the Gajanan Palace. They had been told that *Yuvarani* Sitara was in London for some treatment and she was accompanied by Rituraj Srivastava. That man acted as her bodyguard. Rabri remembered the handsome boy only too well from the time of the wedding. She had also noticed that he was crazy about the princess.

Just now, Rabri put two and two together and arrived at an exact four. The bodyguard must be the cause of the *Yuvaraja's* face being beaten out of shape. No wonder Harischandra was in a black rage. Rabri felt for him. How dare the princess have her bodyguard beat her husband up? After all, even if Harischandra had sent Sitara away, weren't they still man and wife? And hadn't it been a nice gesture on the *Yuvaraja's* part to offer to take his wife back? Shouldn't Sitara Devi be grateful for it?

Rabri grimaced. According to her, Sitara was useless in bed. Harischandra needed a tigress for a partner, the passionate man he was. But what had he got? A kitten instead! Poor man. She felt for him. He would have withered away without her, Rabri, to take care of his needs.

How dare Sitara set her bodyguard on the *Yuvaraja*? Rabri wanted to throttle the princess of Gaekwad with her bare hands. She went down on her knees on the terrace floor, taking his organ into her hands gently before massaging it, her touch turning rougher as she felt his excitement build up. That's when she spoke, confident that she had his ears at that crucial moment, "You should kill them both."

His hands on her head as he pulled her closer to his body, Harischandra replied, "Not kill, no," before he swore, "But I'll have that bodyguard's limbs broken," even as he let out a moan of pleasure.

"And what about the *Yuvarani*?" asked Rabri, biting him hard even as she squeezed his balls.

Harischandra yanked her by the hair, tilting her head far back even as he slapped her across her bared breasts, exactly what she had hoped he would do by invoking his already rampaging temper. "There's no need to do anything. I'm sure her heart will break when she finds out that her lover is a broken man." A maniacal grin split his face as he pushed his cock into her mouth, almost choking her, his diabolical temper blowing out of control when he recalled the way Sitara had laughed when that bastard broke his chin.

He sank back on the couch after some time, totally spent, allowing Rabri to clean him up with a damp cloth before helping him dress. The men he had employed in London to break Rituraj's bones had been unable to do anything. The bodyguard had managed to beat them up to pulp. But then, there had been only three of them and they had been weak foreigners. The next time round, Harischandra would make sure to employ ten strong men, all *desi* locals, built like oxen. And no, he didn't plan to kill the man. That would be too easy. He would have Rituraj's limbs broken into pieces. Harischandra lifted his head to grin again, reaching out a hand to envelope Rabri's breast in a brutal hold. He planned to send the pieces to Sitara in a gift parcel.

Sly as a fox, Harischandra decided to bide his time. He was in no hurry. He'd strike at the worst possible point in their lives. In the meanwhile, he'd let them believe that everything was fine. First things first! The divorce should be gotten out of the way. It would also ensure Harischandra would remain uninvolved from any trouble the police might choose to create.

Now, that was some plan indeed!

19

London, 2002

Rituraj brought two mugs of tea and placed them on the low table in front of Sitara. "It's piping hot," he warned the princess of Gaekwad with a smile on his face. While Rituraj preferred tea which could scald his tongue, he knew that she waited for it to cool down before sipping from it.

Sitara gave him a nod. "I'll wait. But you carry on," she said before continuing to read from her novel.

Rituraj took a mug and began to sip from it, eyeing her. She looked much better than the time when they arrived in London three months ago. The sessions with the psychiatrist, Dr. Gerard King, had done her world of good. She was eating better—he could vouch for that—and was even sleeping better, she said. They were to fly back to India after three more weeks.

It had been both a pleasure and pain, living here in the London apartment which the Raja had rented for them. It was a service apartment, someone coming in twice a week to keep it spic and span. Rituraj did all the cooking and washing. There was a washing machine and dishwasher to make his life easier. Princess Sitara had no clue about housework. Not that it bothered Rituraj one little bit. He was only too happy to do everything for her, making her life smoother. It didn't really bother him that she seemed to take it for granted.

He had finished his tea by the time she lifted her mug to her lips, her eyes on the book. He leaned back on the sofa, crossing his legs as he watched her, drawing infinite joy from being in her presence. It wasn't as if he didn't have work to do or that he couldn't entertain himself. In fact, he had a far busier day than Sitara who didn't really have anything to do. But this time with her in the early evening, drinking tea together, was seriously precious to him.

Sitara suddenly noticed Rituraj staring at her. "What?" she asked, keeping her novel face down on the sofa beside her. "This tea is really good, Ritu," she continued, not waiting for his reply. It was obvious she wasn't really conscious of him, taking his presence as part of her daily routine.

He gave her a brief nod, acknowledging her comment with a smile on his face. "What would you like for dinner?"

"Shall we go out today?" she asked a question of her own.

"You are bored with my cooking?" he teased her with a smile on his face. He was confidently vain about his culinary skills and he had been serving her a variety of cuisines during their stay in London.

Sitara grinned, wrinkling her nose at him. "Of course not, you idiot. I think you could do with a break. You've been working too hard." While that wasn't the reason why she had suggested they go out, she realised it was but the truth. He was always cooking, cleaning or taking care of her. And the first month, he must have spent many sleepless nights, all because of her. Sitara had had recurring nightmares and was terrified of going to sleep before she completed the first month of sessions with Dr. King. On those nights, Rituraj sat on a chair beside her bed, simply holding her hand. He never seemed to tire of doing things for her. While it might appear that Sitara took it all for granted, she most definitely did not. She truly appreciated Rituraj's selfless service, especially after her life in the Gajanan Palace, being ill-treated by her husband and his lover.

She had offered to help around the house, a few times. But Rituraj had refused point blank. "You get well soon, Sitara. Time enough to take up domestic chores later on." He encouraged her to relax and read, pampering her like the princess she was.

Sitara knew how blessed she was that Rituraj was there for her, as her caretaker and bodyguard. And look at the way he had dealt with her husband; soon-to-be ex. She smiled, thinking of the punch he had dealt Harischandra. It felt so good, watching Rituraj smash his fists into her evil husband's face.

How much the man had hurt her during those twenty-two months she had spent as his wife! Not just physically, but mentally too. The worst were the perversions he made her undergo in bed. It was a threesome most of the time, Rabri playing a major role in it. It revolted Sitara to even think of the atrocities she had undergone at their hands; the things they forced her to do. It had been a heaven-sent opportunity when she escaped Harischandra's clutches. Sitara shuddered, thinking about her life at the Gajanan Palace. The treatment was working well. The feeling of fear which had invaded her insides and settled there gradually disappearing after coming to London. While the proud Princess Sitara had been extra careful not to show her fear in Harischandra's presence, it didn't mean that she hadn't lived with feelings of abject terror. She had quaked every time she was in his presence, especially as night time approached. She had hated Rabri's knowing looks and the nefarious schemes the palace maid concocted night after night for the *Yuvaraja's* pleasure.

What a wicked pair!

Rituraj saw the changing expression on Sitara's face, sensitive to notice the disturbance she was undergoing. "Is something wrong, Sitara?"

She sighed long and loud, giving a small shake of her head. "Not really! It's just the thought of Harry. I wonder when they will stop plaguing me." She looked into his compassionate gaze, her lips drooping in a downward curve. "The treatment sessions with Dr. King have stopped the nightmares, definitely. But how do I stop thinking about Harry and Rabri during my waking hours?" There was a pleading expression on her face, as if she hoped he would be able to help her.

"Er… do you have any plans for your future? Like once we return to Baroda, what do you want to do?"

She shrugged. "I'm not really sure. What do you think? I can read only so much," she said, pointing at the book beside her.

"Hmm. Why don't you complete your education?" he asked, an eyebrow raised in query.

She gave him a surprised look, before light dawned on her face that lit up with a slow smile. She snapped her fingers excitedly. "That's an idea, Ritu. An excellent one, actually." She jumped to her feet and dragged him by the hand. "Come on, let's go celebrate. I'll treat you to dinner."

He grinned, letting her pull him to his feet. "In half an hour?"

She nodded. "Yes."

Half an hour later, Rituraj drove them to The Ivy on West Street. It was a good thing they could get a table immediately on arrival. They were seated in a secluded corner and Sitara promptly ordered a bottle of champagne.

Rituraj gave her an amused look. "Are you sure?"

She shrugged nonchalantly. "Why not?" She gave him a small wink. "We are both over eighteen."

"That we are."

A waiter brought a silver bucket in which a bottle of French champagne nestled amidst ice cubes. He removed the cork with a flourish and filled two flutes halfway full and placed them in front of the guests.

Sitara lifted her glass in a toast, waiting for Rituraj to pick his. "To you, Ritu!" she said, touching the tip of her flute to his, even as she looked into his eyes. "I wouldn't have come this far without your help."

Ruddy colour ran up Rituraj's lean cheeks, his brown gaze catching fire as he looked deeply into her eyes. She looked beautiful, wearing a silk dress in royal blue that hugged her figure from shoulder to waist before falling in a flared skirt down to her ankle. A necklace of square cut sapphires set in gold surrounded by small diamonds graced her slender throat while matching earrings dangled from her ears. She wore light makeup, making her skin glow in the light of the lamp hanging over their table. "To you, Sitara!" he responded in a choked voice before drinking from his glass.

Sitara tilted her head and drank deeply from her flute, not taking her eyes off him. Rituraj looked amazing in a navy tuxedo and bowtie over a pristine white shirt. She still couldn't wrap her mind around the fact that he had grown taller and broader in the two years she had lived away from home. She had got to know all about his boxing prowess from Harshvardhan who was all admiration for Rituraj's skill in the ring. He had been thin as a reed when she left the Gaekwad Palace to go live with her husband. He must have worked really hard to become a skilled boxer. She wondered at his many talents. He managed their lives so well, cooking all their meals. He served her different cuisines too, leaving her licking her fingers on most days.

"Where did you learn to cook so well?" she asked, following her own train of thought. Their first course had arrived and they tucked into the cauliflower soup and mustard cheddar toasties. The food was good, but nowhere near as phenomenal as what he served at home.

"Huh?" Rituraj paused, his spoon in mid-air on its way to his mouth, obviously surprised at her question. "From Paresh*ji*, who else?" Paresh Joshi was the palace cook.

"Are you serious?" Sitara gave him an amazed look. "Paresh*ji* taught you to cook?"

Rituraj's brown eyes glinted with amusement. "Didn't I just say that?"

She giggled. "I know. Only, I thought he never lets anyone inside his domain." Paresh was extremely fussy and notorious for his temper. The two people who assisted him in the kitchen were trained to follow his instructions to the T or have their ears boxed. And no one dared disturb Paresh while he cooked up a storm. The Raja and Rani put up with his tantrums only because he was the best cook ever and made the most amazing dishes, perfectly flavoured.

Rituraj grinned. "That's true."

Sitara scowled at him. "What's true?"

"What you said just now. He doesn't let anyone within his domain." He continued to grin as he munched on a toastie. "This is delicious."

She gave him an absentminded nod, keen to know how he had persuaded the palace cook to teach him. "Very funny! Then how did he let you in?"

Rituraj shrugged. "It took a lot of persuasion, of course." He made it sound easy, but it hadn't been like that at all. If Paresh had shooed Rituraj out of his kitchen once, he had done it a hundred times. But how much ever he was scolded, the young man had been determined to learn from the best. Finally, the cook hadn't been left with a choice when Rituraj turned up morning, noon and night, offering to assist. Paresh had been impressed by the boy's persistence and finally surrendered.

Sitara was all admiration, truly. "No wonder you cook so well."

He smiled, pouring more champagne into her glass. "I'm glad you like the food I make."

It was one of the main causes for the return of Sitara's appetite which she had lost after her marriage, the delicious dishes that Rituraj prepared especially for her. "Aren't you having any more champagne?" she asked, looking at his empty glass as he sipped from a glass of water.

"Not for me. You forget that I'll be driving us back home."

The waiter came to remove their empty soup bowls and plates before bringing over the second course of Risotto Primavera and beetroot salad. Sitara discussed with him about her studies. "I think I'll finish my BA first. I don't want to go back to my college. Maybe directly from the university? What do you think?" she asked him, forking a spoon of the creamy risotto into her mouth.

"Not a bad idea." Rituraj had got his admission into MBA at the Baroda University. He would be beginning the course once they went back home. "Do you have an idea of what you want to pursue after your degree?" he asked.

"Social work." Sitara was absolutely clear about it. She had suffered too much in her young life. That's what had made her zero in on social work, to help people who really needed it and lacked the means to pull themselves out of their miserable lives. She still wasn't clear how she would go about it. But she intended to find out.

Rituraj was impressed, nodding in agreement. "Great. MS University offers a course called Social Work and Human Resource Management. That'd be ideal for what you want to do."

Her eyes shone with delight as she placed her fork on her empty plate. "Sounds perfect. I want to help as many people as I can during my lifetime."

Would she want to marry again? Rituraj was hesitant to ask the question. After all, she was just recovering from a traumatic marriage and she wasn't even divorced yet.

Sitara answered his unspoken question as she continued discussing her future with him. "I'll never marry again, ever." She shuddered, sipping more champagne. "The horror of my life with Harry will probably haunt me till the end of my life."

Rituraj sighed, his heart plummeting all the way down to his feet, his dreams going up in smoke. Much to Sitara's surprise, he filled his champagne flute to the brim and throwing back his head, poured it down his throat in one shot.

20

Baroda, 2005

Three days! Three days they lived in a cocoon of bliss, hugging their secret to themselves, sharing surreptitious smiles as they looked at each other across the dining table during meals. They went for lengthy walks, even longer rides on their horses, making prolonged and lazy love during the balmy September nights, forgetting their sorrow over the twin deaths in the family as they found solace in each other's arms.

Neither of them said much, not giving a name to their relationship, not really caring if it would lead to something permanent.

Rituraj refused to think too far into the future, enjoying what was on offer. It was ecstatic, going to sleep and waking up in her arms, no questions asked. Even if they managed to get back to their own beds by early morning, it still gave them a lot of time to make love.

Sitara couldn't believe the turn her life had taken. In the beginning, she had felt secure and loved by her parents. Though Manvendra Singh and Vasundhara Devi were typical Indian royals, they had never felt bad about their firstborn being a daughter. They had adored her from the day she was born and Sitara had been a cherished child.

All that had changed when she got married to Harischandra Gajanan. While his parents treated her with love and respect, the torture she suffered at her husband's hands was disgusting and pathetic. It was only her pride as the princess of Gaekwad which kept her going during those days.

It was a completely shattered Sitara who had returned to the Gaekwad Palace after her failed marriage. It had taken a few months of psychiatric treatment and counselling before Sitara could pick up the reins of her life.

Just as she grabbed at life with both hands and returned to university, the abrupt deaths of both her parents threw her off course. The grief had hit her terribly when Harshvardhan went back to the USA after the funeral rites were completed.

Finally, Sitara found peace in Rituraj's arms. It was like going back home. He cherished her and healed her with his love and attention. Only three days, but it seemed like a lifetime of healing happened during that time. She felt reborn in his arms; her self-worth restored completely.

"It's been two weeks since I went for my boxing practice." Rituraj told Sitara on the fourth morning. "Vinayak Master sent me a message," he grinned, touching her soft cheek with a gentle finger. "He tells me that I'll turn rusty if I don't get back to the ring soon."

Sitara laughed, lifting her face for his kiss, running a hand over his washboard abs. "He might be right. I think you should go. And when will you be back?" He couldn't be going away for more than a few hours, but she was going to miss him, terribly.

Rituraj bent down to kiss her again before replying, "In three or four hours, max. Will you miss me?" They had been inseparable the past few days.

She gave him a nod before burying her face in his chest, her arms closing around his lean waist.

It was a while before Rituraj could prise himself away from her as both of them were equally reluctant to part ways.

They were lying in wait for him, outside the Garodia Boxing Academy. Bansi, the leader of the gang, along with four of his strongest thugs, sat on a wall opposite the academy, keeping a lookout for Rituraj Srivastava to turn up.

Harischandra Gajanan had never forgotten the way Rituraj had bashed his face in London. When he got to know about the sudden death of the Raja and Rani of Gaekwad, he decided to seek vengeance. That's when he had hired Bansi and his thugs to beat his enemy up, an enemy who was too strong to be handled by Gajanan personally.

Bansi had spent a considerable amount of time in gleaning details about his victim. He did his homework thoroughly, finding out all there was to know about Rituraj. He got to know that the younger man, though an amateur, had become a skilled boxer. Bansi chose the strongest and most violent of his men to assist him on his project. He also found out that the Gaekwad Palace had been fortified with alarm systems, and additional security guards. Rituraj didn't trust Harishchandra and preferred playing it safe. The incident in London had made Rituraj realise he was dealing with a sadistic maniac. Bansi decided it was best not to take on Rituraj up there at the palace. That's when he decided to deal with him outside the boxing academy.

They had been waiting for Rituraj to turn up for a few days now, after all the death ceremonies for the Gaekwad royals had been completed.

Bansi sat up, all alert when Rituraj slowed his motorbike outside the academy gates. He nodded to his men, lifting a hand to stop them when they would have walked forward. "He's our man. But let's wait for him to finish his practice. He'll be tired after two to three hours of vigorous exercise. That's when we'll draw him out to the garage."

His men nodded their heads in unison. There was an unused garage about a hundred metres away from the academy. This was to be the location for the brutal assault.

A couple of hours later, an energised Rituraj stepped out of the academy. In a cheerful and relaxed state of mind. He gunned his bike, but it refused to start. Unaware that his assailants had meddled with the spark plugs, he got off the bike and pushed down the kickstand. He didn't anticipate the wooden club which came at him from the back, yelling loudly when it struck the back of his head. He fell down heavily on his front, over the bike, pushing it down and falling over it. Before he could turn over, he felt hands lifting him up in the air and people racing with him down the road. He was totally dazed but still had the presence to call out to Vinayak Garodia.

Bansi and his men threw Rituraj inside the garage, shutting the door and bolting it from the inside before beating him with clubs. He was in no state to fight, blood pouring from his head all the way down his back. It wasn't long before he fainted, unaware that his boxing master and the other students were already breaking down the garage door.

In the span of a few minutes, Vinayak and his boys made mincemeat of Bansi and his men. One of the younger boys had shown tremendous presence of mind and summoned both the police and an ambulance. Soon, the thugs were taken away, each one of them bleeding profusely. Rituraj was rushed to a private hospital in the ambulance. No one noticed his mobile phone which was lying on the floor of the garage, smashed to smithereens.

Sitara Devi was waiting eagerly for Rituraj. When he didn't return by lunch time she tried his mobile number. It was unreachable. That's when she panicked. Just as she was trying to get a contact to the boxing instructor, one of the students called and informed her that Rituraj was in hospital. She had been trying to reach his phone and instinctively knew something was wrong.

Sitara turned pale on receiving the call before rushing out of the palace and getting into a car. "Take me to the Alkapuri Orthopaedic Centre," she told Gajraj, the driver, adding, "As fast as you can." Pressing her sari *pallu* over her mouth, Sitara did her best to control the sobs which attempted to tear through her throat. No! Nothing must happen to Rituraj. He had to stay alive. It didn't occur to her that she was overreacting. But it was so soon after the deaths of her parents and Sitara felt as if the pall of death was building a shroud around her.

She jumped out of the car the moment it came to a stop at the entrance. Vinayak met her there and escorted her to the allotted room. "How bad is it?"

"Better than what I expected," said Vinayak, as they climbed the stairs to the first floor.

Which told her precisely nothing! "What happened?" she asked, her voice wobbly with unshed tears.

"Some thugs beat him up. This happened just outside my boxing academy. I heard Rituraj shout and rushed to his help along with some other students."

"Thugs!" Sitara frowned heavily. "Why would they want to hurt Rituraj? He has no enemies."

"Are you sure? What about your ex-husband? *Yuvaraja* Harischandra Gajanan?" asked Vinayak bitterly. He was terribly upset that his star student had been beaten up so badly. The police had managed to dig up this much information from Bansi—that they had been hired by the Gajanan prince.

Sitara held on to the wooden balustrade, feeling faint, her face turning paler than ever. Oh my God! Poor Rituraj! Would there never be a respite from her ex-husband? Couldn't she live her life peacefully even after they were divorced?

"Are you alright, Princess Sitara?" asked Vinayak, concern in his face and voice as he looked at the young woman leaning against the handrail halfway up the staircase, having come to a stop as if her feet couldn't carry her any further.

She took a deep breath before climbing on to the next step with great effort. "I'm alright, Master Vinayak. How is he?" she asked, a tremor in her voice.

"Apart from having the back of his head smashed in and two fractures, one on his left arm and another on his right shin, he seems to be alright. They are fixing his bones as we talk." Taking her hand in his when he saw that she was once again on the verge of fainting, Vinayak continued, "Believe me, he's not all that bad, considering the bashing he received. It's a wonder nothing else got smashed." He had been worried about the young man's ribs, but it looked like they were safe.

"And you say he's better than what you expected?" Sitara tried her best to tone down the sarcasm in her voice, but it spilled over despite her effort.

Vinayak gave her an unexpected smile, glad to know that the Gaekwad princess had some deep feelings for his student. "Believe me, yes. Those guys were really at it when I arrived on the scene within barely a few minutes. But there were five of them." He frowned, his anger resurfacing. "Bastards!" Then he dashed off, embarrassed at having used foul language in the presence of a princess.

It was more than an hour before Rituraj was wheeled into the room. Sitara, who had been waiting in the corridor outside, walked into the hospital room, her eyes huge as she stared at her lover. Not just her lover, but the love of her life. He seemed to be completely swathed in bandages, one covering the top of his head like a white turban. His eyes were swollen and shut. There was a cast on both his left arm and right leg. Damn Harischandra to hell! Sitara cursed him from the depths of her heart.

Not really bothered about Vinayak and the other students who hovered around, Sitara went to sit on the chair next to the bed and took Rituraj's right hand in hers. It felt limp, so unlike his otherwise firm hold. She wasn't aware of the tears pouring down her cheeks as she stared at his face as she willed him to get better.

Baroda, 2006

It was about three months later when Rituraj could finally get rid of his crutches. Sitara had never left his bedside during the two weeks he spent in the hospital, going to the palace for a few hours every other day only when Vinayak twisted her arm to do so.

"I don't want two patients on my hands, you see. Or should I ask the hospital staff to add another bed here along with an IV connection?" Vinayak wasn't laughing when he made the suggestion. She had lost weight within the first three days of Rituraj's sojourn in the hospital. Was the princess eating at all? But Sitara was so obviously strong, mentally. She kept a strict vigil on Rituraj, making sure that he was as comfortable as possible under the circumstances.

"I don't want to leave his side," she protested, her eyes on the patient even though she was speaking to Vinayak.

The boxing master sighed deeply. *As if I don't know!* "But you must agree that you can only take care of him if you are fit and healthy yourself," he insisted in a gentle voice. "Go and rest for a few hours. I promise to remain by your Rituraj's side; won't move an inch away. I'll wait for your return before even going to the bathroom," he said, grinning at her.

Sitara shook her head at him. "Please Master*ji*! He's not *my* Rituraj. Don't ever call him that," she said in a fierce whisper, turning away from the patient and walking towards Vinayak who was standing at the foot of Rituraj's bed.

Vinayak raised an eyebrow in query. "Are you sure about that?"

"That's how it has to be," she insisted. She walked to the door, gesturing for Vinayak to follow her. She had been thinking about this since the time Rituraj was beaten up by Harischandra's thugs. Rituraj would never agree with her decision. But Vinayak was older and more mature. He must surely understand. "It's better that Rituraj stays away from me. Or there's no saying what my ex-husband will do. He's the devil incarnate, through and through. And he's like a dog in the manger; *woh aisa insaan hai jo eent ka jawab patthar se deta hai.* Rituraj did gleefully throw the first brick by bashing him up in London. Harry would continuously create trouble until he avenges his defeat. Even more importantly, I should stay away from Rituraj."

And make a sacrifice of your life, forever! And Rituraj's also into the bargain! Vinayak didn't say the words as he gave her a bitter yet empathetic look. He couldn't help but agree with what she said. But will Rituraj accept it? Most definitely not. But then, wasn't that one of the reasons why he was well-respected by everyone, including Vinayak himself?

Vinayak shrugged now. "Can't we find a better solution to this?" he asked, unable to think of anything.

Sitara shook her head. "You tried to lodge a complaint against Harry based on Bansi's statement, right?" When Vinayak nodded, she continued, "What happened after that?"

Vinayak shook his head. "The Indore police buried the case."

"Exactly. That's the kind of power Harischandra wields. He has the police, the government machinery and even respectable High Court judges in his pocket. You can't reason with him nor can you fight him. There's no way to escape him."

Vinayak didn't like what he was hearing, though he couldn't argue with what she said. "I'm sure Rituraj…"

"Master*ji*!" Sitara placed a hand on Vinayak's arm, stopping him mid-sentence. "Please don't say anything to Rituraj. I will not have his life compromised under any circumstance." Her voice had gone up by several notches now that they were outside Rituraj's room and she wanted to drive her point home. Grimacing, she lowered her tone to say, "Please Master*ji*, promise me that you won't mention anything to him." She extended her right hand to him, palm upwards, her grey eyes pleading.

"Okay, I'll promise, on one condition."

"What?" asked Sitara, a frown on her face as she glared at the boxing master.

Vinayak grinned triumphantly. "That you go to the palace to rest for a few hours every other day."

"But…"

Vinayak shrugged. "It's all up to you."

"Mmm." Her hand was still extended.

"What was that? I didn't hear." His voice shook with laughter.

Sitara gritted her teeth, glaring at the stubborn Vinayak. "Okay, I'll go."

"Go where? When?" Vinayak wanted everything clear and precise. He felt responsible for Sitara when her Man Friday was laid up bruised and battered in the hospital bed. She could do with plenty of caring, nurturing.

"Master*ji*!" Sitara's voice came out in a screech before she paused to take a deep breath. "I'll do as you say. I'll go to the palace every alternate day to rest for a few hours. Okay? Now give me your promise."

Vinayak gave her a broad smile which softened his rugged features. Placing a hand on her palm, he said, "I promise not to talk to Rituraj about what you told me just now." He crossed the fingers of his left hand behind his back. Only, Sitara didn't get a chance to see it, just the way he meant it to be.

"Thank you, Master*ji*."

"You go home now. I'll stay with Rituraj until you return."

While Sitara didn't care for the idea of leaving Rituraj's bedside, she realised she didn't really have a choice and went home to the palace. But the break did her good, enough to make her appreciate Vinayak's gesture. It also gave her more energy to care for Rituraj.

Sitara had the room next to the palace library converted into a bedroom for Rituraj on the ground floor. The pretext was that it would be difficult for him to climb the stone staircase with forty-five steep steps all the way up to his bedroom on the first floor, since the ceiling was high. But she was actually distancing herself from him.

She went to see him at those times when she knew for a fact that he was fast asleep. He was given sleeping tablets for the first month. But after that, he stopped taking the dose, insisting he didn't need them. He stopped the painkillers after two more weeks. The doctor went along with Rituraj's idea only because his patient was young at twenty-four and also extremely fit. Still Rituraj had to use crutches and completely rest his right leg for a minimum period of three months. They had put a steel rod and a couple of wires to knit the tibia which had broken to smithereens.

That night, Rituraj was wide awake when Sitara went to see him at eleven. She was sure he must be fast asleep, unaware that he had stopped taking the sleeping tablet. "Hey!"

Sitara stopped in her tracks, her shocked grey gaze meeting his alert brown one. He should have been deeply asleep. Brijmohan had informed her that Rituraj had taken all his medicines after dinner. How come he wasn't asleep by now?

"Hello!" she greeted him, her voice a hoarse whisper. "How have you been?"

"I've been missing you terribly. Come here!" he commanded, lifting his right hand and crooking a finger at her.

"I'm fine right where I am," she said, straightening her shoulders and folding her arms across her chest.

He got up to sit on his bed, turning to his right and attempting to get out of the bed.

"Stop it, Rituraj!" she called out, her voice sharp. With great difficulty, she forced down the anxiety that churned in her stomach. She didn't want him to suffer a setback. "The doctor has given strict orders for you to stay put in bed."

Leaning back against the bedhead, he said, "Why don't you come closer? I need a kiss." While he vaguely recalled her presence next to his bed in the hospital, he never got to see her after returning to the palace. And how much he missed her! Her warmth, her proximity, her softness and her kisses.

Sitara shook her head firmly, her heart hammering against her chest. She so wanted to rush over and gather him into her arms, kissing him senseless. Despite all the battering he had suffered at the thugs' hands, Rituraj looked so damn attractive. Wasn't he lucky that the bone structure on his face hadn't been affected! And just because she wanted to maintain distance between them didn't mean that she had stopped loving him.

But no! It won't do to show any emotion towards him. She had to somehow convince him that those three days of togetherness was a complete sham. She tilted her chin, putting on her royal airs and looked at him down her sharp nose. "Why don't you go to sleep, Rituraj? Or should I call the doctor?"

"What's with the full name?" he grumbled, "Why don't you call me Ritu as you always do?"

She pretended not to hear him. "Do you want me to send for Brijmohan? Maybe he can help you see a movie on the DVD player."

"Sitara? Is something wrong?" he asked, turning to place both his feet on the floor, preparing to walk to her.

Sitara's heart beat so hard that she felt choked, panic setting in as she watched him helplessly. He was not to attempt walking without assistance. And she refused to go anywhere near him. All her willpower would go up in smoke if she went within a few feet of Rituraj. And she could not do that to him. She didn't think he would survive another attack by Harischandra's goons.

"Rituraj! I think you should stay put in bed. I'll go get Brijmohan." She fled.

Rituraj frowned heavily. This simply wasn't the behaviour of the woman who had melted in his arms more than a month ago. She couldn't have enough of him. So much so that he had been sure Sitara was in love with him. Okay, maybe not to the same extent he loved her, but she definitely had feelings for him. What had happened since then?

Okay, he'd been beaten up and broken a few bones. Shouldn't that have brought her closer to him instead of rejecting him outright? His scowl turned blacker when Brijmohan walked in. "You want to watch a film, Rituraj sir?"

"Stop calling me sir," he snarled at the palace servant. "How many times have I told you to simply call me Rituraj?

Brijmohan smiled indulgently at the patient. He loved the boy far too much to feel hurt by his words. "*Arre baba*! That was when you were a child. I can't simply call you by your name now that you are managing the palace, plus you are Princess Sitara's assistant. I am merely a lowly servant here."

"*Aap bhi na*, Brijmohan*ji*!" Rituraj shook his head at the other man who gently pushed him back on the bed. "I want to get up. I need to talk to Sitara."

"Not now, you can't. The princess has retired for the night." Brijmohan pulled the comforter over Rituraj.

"Bullshit! What nonsense is this? Sitara was right here in this room just a few minutes ago."

"Of course, the princess was here," replied Brijmohan patiently. "She only told me that you needed help and that she was retiring for the night." He spoke as if he was addressing a child, angering Rituraj all the more.

He waited in vain over two more days for the princess to visit him. But she never did. By the end of the second day, he was ready to climb the wall in frustration. Why was she shunning him? There had to be a reason. He knew Sitara only too well. While she had turned to him in her grief, it wasn't long before she wanted to make love to him as much as he wanted it. What had happened now to keep her away from him?

While Vinayak hadn't said much, the other students told Rituraj about how Princess Sitara had insisted on staying with him in the hospital, refusing to even rest for brief periods until Vinayak had pushed her into a corner.

When had she stopped seeking his company? *After I came home and began to stay awake for longer hours.* Rituraj frowned deeper than ever. Did that mean she didn't want him anymore? Simply not possible! Sitara wasn't some society butterfly flitting from relationship to relationship. She wouldn't have given herself to him for a lark.

It was too bloody confusing. And why had she addressed him by his full name? She hadn't bothered to reply when he asked her outright. In a flash of temper, Rituraj lifted the table lamp and threw it across the room at the door connecting to the library, not caring when it smashed to pieces.

Sitara, who had been working in the library, rushed to Rituraj's room when she heard the noise.

Rituraj smiled in satisfaction when he saw the worried look on her face. "Thanks for coming, Princess Sitara," he greeted her sarcastically; "I've been trying to meet you for some days now."

"Is it something important, Rituraj? I'm rather busy. You know the amount of work I have. And with my assistant laid up, it's getting more difficult to manage each day." Her hands were clenched into tight fists at her sides, her feet planted firmly at the door as she held herself back with great difficulty. NO! *I will not throw myself into his arms!*

"Why the hell don't you let your assistant do his job?" he asked, abject frustration in his voice. If that was the only way she was going to let him get close, so be it!

"I need a fitness certificate from his doctor," she said firmly, refusing to meet his eyes.

"You'll get it by the end of the day, I swear."

"I'll take your leave in that case," she said, turning to the door.

"Sitara…" There was a wealth of emotion in his voice as he called her, his arms aching with the need to have them around her.

"You get the certificate, Rituraj. And let's get you back to work after that." She almost ran away, unable to bear his proximity.

Baroda, 2006

It was sheer torture working next to her in the library, Sitara continuing to call Rituraj by his full name. She was ready to discuss anything concerning work. But when it came to personal issues, the princess simply clammed up and behaved as if she was short of hearing.

As his pain reduced and the movement in his limbs improved, Rituraj faced abject frustration in her proximity. How he missed his boxing classes! Talking of which, he was yet to deal with Harischandra Gajanan. He had nothing to say to the hired goons. They had, after all, been doing their job. But Gajanan couldn't get away scot free.

Cold showers seemed to be an answer. Rituraj also took up meditation. His boxing master told him deep breathing helped the body, the mind and the soul. While the frustrated Rituraj wanted to show Vinayak his middle finger, he decided to give it a try as his girlfriend of three days seemed to have ditched him forever, without giving him a reason for it.

And the sucker for punishment that he was, Rituraj wasn't ready to walk away from Sitara. He didn't care if she wanted him or not. He was there for her, always—as a friend, assistant, bodyguard—in whatever capacity she needed him; and whenever.

Sitara gave him a look from the corner of her eyes as Rituraj sat near the window, the sunlight falling on him giving the appearance of a halo as he worked on his laptop. He was barely a few feet away. If she took a few steps forward, she would just fall into his arms. And she knew that he would take her, no questions asked. She was sure of his unconditional love for her. She turned her head away to sniff, controlling the tears waiting to gush out of her eyes. No way! No way was she going to place his life in danger, ever again.

Being a shrewd princess and aware of how the royal grapevine worked, she set the rumour mill in motion that Rituraj Srivastava was only a manager at the Gaekwad Palace; an employee of the royal household and nothing beyond that.

The next step was to shift him to the outhouse where Rituraj lived originally when his parents were alive. Not keen to hurt him, Sitara was wondering how go about it. Of course, he was bound to get hurt. She sighed deeply now, straightening her back and tilting her chin in determination. They could not stay under the same roof. It was too much temptation for both of them. For another, the rumour she had floated, needed to be corroborated. Harischandra was bound to have it checked and it would simply fall apart if he found that Sitara and Rituraj lived under the same roof.

Anyway, she had a valid excuse now. With her parents gone, and Harshvardhan studying abroad, it wasn't right if she and Rituraj continued to live in the palace. It was bound to create gossip.

Why can't we simply get married? Won't that shut up every single gossipmonger? Sitara gritted her teeth to control her roiling emotions. Of course, they couldn't get married. Not if she wanted Rituraj to remain safe from Harischandra. Her ex-husband was a snake and she didn't want the man she loved to end up as a dead body all because of Harischandra's spite. No, marriage to Rituraj wasn't on the cards, not with the demoniac Harischandra hale and hearty.

Getting Rituraj to move to the outhouse was the answer. She would do it even if it killed her.

An angry scowl on his face, Rituraj held the new servant by his ear, just enough for the younger man to feel pain. "What's your name?" It was the first time in years that he didn't know the name of someone who had stepped into the Gaekwad Palace. The man must have been hired while he was in the hospital.

"Shantaram, *sahib*." While the guy answered firmly, there was a trace of fear on his face.

"Do you work in the palace?" The question came out like a gunshot.

"*Ji!* My *mausi* is distantly related to Nirupama aunty's friend. She…"

Rituraj lifted a hand to shut the boy—yes, he seemed to be barely eighteen—up, before asking, "What are you doing here?" Shantaram had been standing outside the library window, his head tilted as if he had been listening to something.

"Nothing, *sahib*. I came to ask the princess if she wanted her clothes ironed."

Rituraj's scowl grew heavier on hearing the boy's reply. It was Nirupama's duty to take care of Sitara's clothes. The loyal maid had all of them washed and pressed before hanging them in the princess's wardrobe. For one thing, in all these years he had known her, Sitara had never sent her clothes to be ironed. For another, why come to her work place to ask for her clothes? Something wasn't in sync. Though young, Shantaram had a glib tongue it seemed. Rituraj perceived that immediately, his hackles raised.

After the attack by Harischandra Gajanan's goons, Rituraj realised that he needed to be extra careful, especially with a new servant recently employed by the palace. He wondered what the need had been to hire someone at this juncture when both the Raja and Rani had passed on. The work should be less for obvious reasons. Why did they need a new servant at all? He had better get to the bottom of it.

"Where do you come from?" asked Rituraj.

"Baroli in Madhya Pradesh."

That did it. Baroli was a village not far from Indore. Rituraj immediately concluded that Shantaram must have been sent by Harischandra Gajanan. With Rituraj in hospital and Sitara attending on him, it was the perfect time to send someone to infiltrate the palace. Who must have authorised hiring the boy? He must speak to Brijmohan regarding it.

"You had better go and help in the kitchen, do you hear? The older servants will take care of the princess's needs."

"*Ji sahib*," said Shantaram, lowering his gaze respectfully before walking away.

What must Harischandra want to know that he had sent a spy over to the Gaekwad Palace? He was the one who had shunned Sitara and sent her back to her parents. He was the one who had sought divorce and got it too. While the divorce had done Sitara a world of good, it seemed to have made her ex-husband want to wreck up her life all the more.

Rituraj could sort of accept why Harischandra had sent his thugs after him. The Gajanan *Yuvaraja* must have been biding his time to seek revenge after the way Rituraj had hit him in London, not once but twice. Not having the guts to deal with him directly to his face, the Gajanan rat had sent his henchmen after Rituraj. All that was fine. But sending his man to the Gaekwad Palace to spy on Sitara Devi was totally cheap and uncouth. What did Gajanan expect to achieve by doing that? Was he planning to harm Sitara in some way?

Why bother? Rituraj bunched up his fist in frustration before sitting down heavily on a wooden bench in the garden. He liked to pace while thinking. But right now, it wasn't really practical limping around with his crutches.

Why the hell had Gajanan sent his spy to work at the Gaekwad Palace? Rituraj was worried for Sitara's safety. One thing he was clear though: he didn't want to talk to her about it.

Rituraj was glad when Vinayak visited him later in the evening. "Hello, Master*ji*, how have you been?"

Vinayak laughed, patting Rituraj on his right shoulder. "I've never been better. You tell me, how are you?"

"Not too bad. But listen. I want to run something by you." Rituraj quickly told Vinayak about Shantaram.

"Why would Harischandra want to send his spy over here? Do you think he is planning to harm Sitara Devi in some way?"

Vinayak frowned. Sitara had told him all about how Gajanan's mind worked. But she had also taken his promise not to tell Rituraj anything about it. Then again, she didn't know about the spy in Gaekwad Palace. "Are you going to tell the princess about the new servant who's Harischandra's spy?" he asked Rituraj.

Rituraj frowned, shaking his head slowly from side to side. "She's undergone a lot pf trauma in the past few years. I don't want to burden her any further. I…"

"I agree." Vinayak gave him a nod. He paused for a few seconds, making his peace with his conscience before plunging in, "Okay, I'm not all that good at keeping promises; not if it's at the stake of the happiness of people I like. Sitara is worried about Harischandra attacking you, all because you are close to her." There, he had said it, broken his promise to the Gaekwad princess. Vinayak gave a mental shrug. There wasn't much else he could do under the circumstances, not with Rituraj and Sitara worrying about each other, all because of that blackguard Gajanan.

Rituraj sighed heavily, not really surprised to hear of Sitara's thoughts about the attack. No wonder she had been avoiding him as if he was down with some highly contagious disease. As for Rituraj, he had his own suspicions which were probably closer to the truth. Speaking to Vinayak about it, he said, "I don't think that's the reason. He must have sent his goons to beat me up because I beat him when he visited us in London."

Vinayak was surprised, both his eyebrows raised in query. "When did that happen? When you escorted Sitara Devi to London some years ago?"

Rituraj nodded. "Yes. The bastard came to the apartment, ordering Sitara to go back and live with him once again."

"Bastard indeed! He has some guts for sure."

"Not really." Rituraj grinned at his boxing master. "Harischandra likes to throw his weight around on those who are weaker than him. He took the beating I gave him and slunk away like a typical rat."

"Only to send his goons after you." Vinayak had a worried look in his eyes now. Did that mean Rituraj could never live in peace? No wonder Princess Sitara Devi was worried. It looked like she knew her ex-husband only too well. Wasn't it a good thing he had broken his promise to her and warned Rituraj?

Rituraj shrugged. "This isn't the first time. He sent some *firang* thugs after me in London a couple of days after I smashed his jaw. They were no match for me, of course." His off-hand statement didn't sound vain, just matter-of-fact.

Vinayak puffed up with pride at his student's achievement. though. "How many of them?" he asked.

"Three men, built like gorillas." Rituraj's grin became wider.

"And?"

"I made mincemeat out of them." He gave Vinayak a broad wink.

Vinayak guffawed. "Good for you." He grimaced the next second, his laughter disappearing. "This isn't funny, Rituraj. We need to take some kind of legal action against Gajanan. Or you will never be at peace. Nor can the princess. Especially if your guess about his sending a spy into the palace is valid."

Rituraj grimaced. "I'll go with my gut and swear that Shantaram is a spy. I'll gather proof before taking any action though. And I think you are absolutely right regarding Gajanan. We definitely need to do something. So, listen; here's my plan." Rituraj quickly explained his idea to Vinayak, who nodded in encouragement as he listened to the younger man, not interrupting him till the end.

"Excellent! It might just work," said Vinayak, giving the plan his approval.

"It had better work," said Rituraj, a determined thrust to his square chin. "Can I rely on you to send a couple of your best boys? I need Sitara watched round the clock."

"I can send you my second and third best, of course. You know very well you are my best student, Rituraj," said Vinayak, a serious expression on his face.

Rituraj gave the other man a smart salute. "Thanks Master*ji*."

"It's only the truth. Let me talk to Deven and Kamal. I'm sure they'll be only too eager to help."

"Perfect. Thank you so much, Master*ji*."

"You do realise that I also want to bring an end to this threat, don't you?" Vinayak grumbled, genuinely worried for Rituraj and Sitara Devi.

"But of course." Rituraj got up and shook hands with his boxing master.

"First things first, Rituraj. I think it's best you shift out of the palace. Is there somewhere nearby where you live and keep an eye on Sitara Devi?"

Rituraj sighed, not caring for the idea but agreeing with Vinayak. "I will move into the outhouse tomorrow itself. It's in the palace compound and will keep me as close to Sitara as possible without the two of us living under the same roof."

Rituraj limped his way into the library the next morning with the help of his crutches. "Good morning, Princess Sitara." Of course, he was formal, dammit! She hadn't left him with a choice, had she? She looked so graceful as she sat at her father's desk, working on the laptop. Her hair was tied in a loose knot at the nape of her neck while she was draped in a rich cream chiffon sari which magnificently enhanced her golden skin.

Sitara lifted her head to look at him, desire inadvertently leaping into her grey eyes and glowing there for a few seconds before she pulled the shutters down. Rituraj hadn't missed the play of emotions on her face. That she had feelings for him was something he now took safely for granted. His heart took wing, fluttering joyfully in his chest. But he had better not change his mind now. He had no choice but to shift out of the palace and into the outhouse.

"Good morning, Rituraj!" responded Sitara only after a couple of minutes as she struggled to bring her emotions under control. Her heart raced a mile a minute as she caught the passion in his gaze. She sat there and with sheer will power, blanked out her mind.

He walked forward to sit on the visitor's chair opposite her, leaning his crutches against the desk. "I have decided to move into the outhouse."

Sitara's mouth fell open. Okay, she had wanted him to do exactly that. But wasn't she the one making the decisions around here? How come he had decided to shift to the outhouse? She frowned at him, all set to argue.

Rituraj lifted a hand to stop her from saying anything. "Don't stop me, Princess Sitara. Let me be honest. I won't survive living in the palace along with you, not after the way we made love during those three days. I don't know if you're aware how difficult it is for me to control my hands. When I look at you all I want to do is to hold you, kiss you and make love to you." His voice was hoarse with emotion as he looked at her from across the table, adoringly.

Sitara's toes curled on the carpet as she clenched her hands at her sides. It was an effort not to jump off her chair and throw herself into his arms. She wished she had never set eyes on Harischandra. He was the one who stood between her and her true love. She turned her face away, not wanting Rituraj to see the expression in her eyes. *Of course, I'm aware, you idiot. It's difficult for me too, to keep my hands off you. As for my heart, it's already in your keeping.* The words were a silent scream inside her. But there was simply no way she could utter them, not if she wanted to keep Rituraj safe.

Rituraj was shaken by the deep sense of disappointment he felt when she turned her face away.

But somehow, he refused to believe she had no feelings for him. Maybe it was way too soon after her parents' deaths. And her divorce was also fairly recent. Sitara was young, after all, and must be worried about what the world would say. Rituraj placed a hand against the left side of his chest as if to calm down his aching heart, before sitting up straight. Patience was the key! And some distance!

There was also the point Vinayak had mentioned last night. Sitara was probably under the impression that Harischandra would attack if she got close to Rituraj. Somehow, Rituraj didn't take that threat too seriously. He was convinced Harischandra had staged the attack as retaliation for the humiliating manner in which he had been beaten up by Rituraj.

Rituraj continued to speak when Sitara didn't say anything. "I'd like to carry on working as your assistant, if you have no objection. Though I insist on being your bodyguard." He gave a self-deprecating smile. "I know that I'm unfit as I am, but this is all temporary. I'll be one hundred per cent fit in a few months. In the meanwhile, Vinayak Master and a couple of his students will keep an eye out for you."

Sitara turned back to stare at him, her eyes going wide on hearing those last words. "What's the need…?"

"There's every need. Harischandra Gajanan is dangerous with a capital D. I don't want him to harm you in any way." Rituraj's voice was firm when he uttered those words.

Sitara grimaced. *And I don't want him to harm you in any way.* And while it was she who had wanted Rituraj out of the palace, it didn't mean she liked the idea at all, especially now that *he* had suggested it. But did they really have a choice?

With a sad heart, Sitara nodded, agreeing to everything he suggested. Wasn't she lucky that he wanted to continue working with her? Both as her assistant and her bodyguard?

Sitara realised that she might simply have killed herself otherwise.

Indore, 2007

"**A**re you sure?" Harischandra asked Rabri, his eyes glittering with malice. The maid had just brought in his morning tea and also some news to impart along with it.

"Yes, *Yuvaraja*. That bodyguard has been living in the outhouse since the Raja and Rani of Gaekwad passed on. I…"

"How do you know?"

"My sister-in-law's son has gone to work there in Sitara Devi's palace. I planted him there only because…"

Harischandra lifted an impatient hand, stopping her in mid-sentence. "You told me about that. Is he reliable? Your nephew?"

Rabri nodded her head vigorously, a wide smile on her face. "Of course, *Yuvaraja*. Why would I send him otherwise? He went to work there soon after Rituraj's accident."

"And what did he tell you exactly?" Harischandra eyed her shrewdly as he sipped from his teacup.

"Shantaram told me that Rituraj moved out of the palace from the day he could move around with his crutches."

Harischandra frowned. "Who the hell is Shantaram now?"

The triumphant look on Rabri's face dimmed. She sniffed before answering, "Shantaram is my nephew. I did tell you that he…"

Harischandra lifted his hand again, impatience in every line of his body. He wanted only the essential details while Rabri was wanting to elaborate on trivialities. "Can you just get to the point, Rabri? I don't have all the time in the world."

Rabri was pretty miffed on hearing his harsh words. "That's all," she said.

Harischandra plonked the teacup down on the tray with a thud, getting to his feet. "You came rushing here only to inform me that the bodyguard has moved into the outhouse? What nonsense is this?" he thundered, glaring at her with red-rimmed eyes.

Rabri wasn't one to be scared of *Yuvaraja* Gajanan. She knew exactly which buttons she could push. Lifting her chin up in the air, she said, "That's the news I received from my nephew and I thought you'll be relieved to hear that." She placed the tea jug on the tray before lifting it in her hand, preparing to leave Harischandra's chamber even as she looked at him from the corner of her eyes.

"Why the hell should I care if Rituraj lives in the palace or in hell?" Harischandra snarled at the maid.

Rabri gave an impatient sigh before explaining to him in a tone one would use to address a child. "Can't you see something here, *Yuvaraja*? Sitara Devi and her bodyguard are obviously not lovers as you believed them to be."

"Huh?" The frown left Harischandra's forehead as he stared at Rabri with a surprised look on his face. "Why do you think so?"

"Isn't it obvious? If that were the case, why would he go to live separately when he has been living in the palace all these years?" It was with great difficulty she controlled the sarcasm from spilling over. Sleeping with the *Yuvaraja* tended to make Rabri careless, making her forget her status many a time.

Harischandra rubbed his chin thoughtfully. Could Rabri be right?

"And another thing, *Yuvaraja*," said Rabri, giving him a coy smile, waiting for him to give her his complete attention.

"What?"

"How can you even imagine that Sitara Devi would be satisfied with another man after having you for her husband?" she asked him rhetorically, her voice flattering even as she gave him an adoring look.

Harischandra's anger disappeared like mist at the advent of sunlight as he gave her one of his lascivious grins. "You have a point there, my Rabri. Come here!"

Rabri placed the tray on the table, rushing into his arms, having got him exactly where she wanted him. Who cared about either Sitara Devi or Rituraj? Not she anyway.

24

Baroda, 2009

It took Rituraj almost two years to gather material to use against Harischandra Gajanan, but he ultimately got some excellent photographs, all thanks to a private detective and a bar dancer from Indore.

He gathered as much information as he could about Harischandra and his weaknesses. While the *Yuvaraja* was into drinking and gambling, his main weakness was women. And he was obsessed with sexual perversions.

"Harischandra Gajanan gets a kick out of beating everyone up," said Murli Manohar, the private detective whom Rituraj had hired. "But I see a pattern here. The Gajanan prince shows his might against only those weaker than he is. I don't think he has the guts to face anyone who's stronger than him."

Rituraj nodded in agreement. Hadn't he himself realised that long ago? "Do you have anything more on him?" he asked now, calling the waiter to order two more beers.

Murli smiled, the expression on his face suggesting he had saved the best for the last. "Yes, I do."

"Go on."

"It seems that Harischandra had whipped this woman, a young girl actually, from the red-light area so badly and left her to bleed profusely. She was half-dead when they found her on the floor of her room the next morning. She had to be treated in the hospital for one whole month before she recovered. In the meanwhile, the brothel owner had to spend a lot of money not only on her treatment but it was one more month before she could return to earn her living."

Rituraj frowned. What a horrible man! "Are you saying Harischandra walked away from the shady joint without offering to help?"

Murli laughed sarcastically. "Help? Forget help, he didn't even bother to inform them that the girl was semi-conscious when he left. He's an out and out bastard. And listen, there's more. The woman who runs the brothel is close to some people in the police department. She had made an unofficial complaint and…"

"Why not an official complaint? She had a proper case against him and I'm sure the doctors at the hospital would have been ready to help." Rituraj couldn't help interrupting, his blood boiling with anger.

"One thing you need to know about this man, it's next to impossible to file a FIR against Gajanan Junior. Such is the power he wields. But this time round, the police couldn't simply sit back and let things take their course as the brothel owner threatened to shut her doors to the entire department. It worked. The Assistant Commissioner of Police paid a visit to the Gajanan Palace and had a long talk with Raja Digvijay Gajanan." Murli stopped to sip from his bottle of beer, smacking his lips as he relished the drink.

Rituraj drank from his bottle, waiting impatiently for the detective to continue with his story.

"The Raja threatened to disinherit the *Yuvaraja* if he got into any more scrapes."

"Do you think it's working?" Rituraj had his doubts. But then again, it was two years since he had been beaten up. There had been nothing from Harischandra's side. Just maybe Raja Gajanan had some sort of control over his offspring.

Murli shrugged. "So far, so good. There's no record of any mishaps since that incident."

They ordered dinner, Murli explaining how he went about the whole exercise of gathering material against Harischandra Gajanan.

Rituraj listened, fascinated with what he was hearing. Detective work seemed quite difficult with a lot of slogging while things didn't fall into one's lap as portrayed in most thrillers. Putting his thoughts to words, he asked, "Do you enjoy what you do, Murli?"

Murli grinned. "Absolutely. I've always been a curious kid, poking my nose into things which didn't concern me. Then my hobby, my passion and my career all merged together and ended up in my becoming a sleuth."

"Sounds like a dream come true."

"Believe me, that's exactly what it is."

Rituraj's mind had been in a tizzy from the moment he heard about Raja Gajanan's threat to disinherit his son. Finally, an idea flashed in his mind. Deciding to put that into action, he said to the detective, "Tell me something. There may be no record of any mishap after Digvijay Gajanan's ultimatum. But do you really believe that a leopard would change its spots?"

Murli smiled, shaking his head. "It's not natural."

"Exactly. Can you dig some more?"

"I'll need to dig in really deep. It's going to cost a lot of money."

"You don't worry about that. You get me some really good evidence. Nothing like photographs. Or video recordings. Do you think you can do that?"

Murli sat up straight. "Of course, I can Mr. Srivastava, without a doubt. But I'll need a few months at the least."

Rituraj nodded. "I'll wait for your call."

25

Indore, 2008

“*Y*ou wanted to see me, Father?” Harischandra sat down on a chair across Raja Gajanan’s ornate desk.

Digvijay had been working in his study when he decided to summon his son. He was terribly upset, ashamed actually, after the visit from the district’s Assistant Commissioner of Police. Digvijay Gajanan was highly respected like all of his ancestors before him. All their dealings with the police department had been friendly, so far. But it looked like Harischandra had a terrible reputation…

“*Namaste*, Raja Digvijay Gajanan. Thank you for the audience,” said ACP Selva Durai, bringing both his hands together in greeting.

“Welcome to our palace, ACP Selva Durai. Please take a seat,” said Digvijay before asking curiously, “You don’t seem to be from North India, are you?”

Selva Durai smiled. “No, sir. I am from Tamil Nadu.”

“You must have an excellent reputation for your department to give you a posting here in such a high position.”

Selva Durai cleared his throat. It was time to get down to the purpose of his visit. "Actually, the problem is that no one from the north wants to be posted in senior positions in this city."

The Raja lifted a hand to the servant who poured two cups of tea for both of them, indicating that they should be left alone. Turning to the ACP, he said, "Please help yourself," before responding to the other man's words, "Is there a reason for that?"

Selva Durai gave a small nod, sipping from his teacup. "Yes, and that's why I am here today, seeking an audience with you."

Raja Gajanan saw the serious expression on the other man's face and immediately realised the cause for it. Cursing his son from the bottom of his heart, he portrayed an outward calm, saying, "Please go ahead."

"Let me get straight to the point, sir. Your son's behaviour gives sleepless nights to our whole department. Simply put, he has got most of the policemen in his pocket while the rest of us are too petrified of him to take action. I've been newly appointed here and have been working in Indore for the last five months. They have made me a… what is it you people say in Hindi? A *bakra*. That's it!" The ACP snapped his fingers. "I hope you understand my awkward position." There was no fear in Selva Durai's eyes as he looked directly into the Raja's gaze.

"Don't keep me in suspense, Durai. I do have an idea what my son is capable of. Just give it to me straight," ordered the Raja, placing his empty teacup down on the centre table with extra care even as his hand trembled due to his rising temper.

Selva Durai spoke quickly. "There have been many complaints against the *Yuvaraja*, all the FIRs. torn and flushed down toilets. No one has the guts to bell the cat, while every policeman in Indore has knowledge of all the misdemeanours committed by him. Did you know that there was a police team from Baroda, trying to file a case against your son? They…"

Digvijay Gajanan sat up straighter than before, the name Baroda ringing a loud bell. "What was it regarding?"

"Harischandra Gajanan had hired some goons to beat up Princess Sitara Devi's bodyguard. The man had many broken bones but managed to survive with timely medical intervention. It was one lucky escape."

"Damn!" The Raja turned pale on listening to Selva Durai's words. What levels had his son sunk to?

"But the local police refused to co-operate. The Baroda police were forced to give up and go back. Believe me, what I told you is just one of the many crimes your son has committed. A few months ago, he had beaten up a prostitute, a young woman of barely nineteen years and left her to die at the brothel. It was sheer luck that the girl survived."

"Enough!" The Raja pressed a hand to his chest, unable to bear the shame of the ACP's words. Not for a moment did he even consider that the other man was making false accusations against his son.

Selva Durai got up to go to the Raja's side. "Are you alright, sir? Can I get you something?"

Digvijay Gajanan shook his head, a sad smile on his face. "No, thank you, Selva Durai. Why don't you sit down and allow me a few moments to recover from the shock you have just given me?" While the Raja was fully aware of the cruelty his son was capable of, he still found it difficult to digest that Harischandra could be so heartless. How could he simply leave the woman bleeding and walk away from the scene as if nothing had happened? What in case she had actually died? The Raja felt shaken to the core of his being.

The ACP went back to sit down across his host and kept his silence, waiting for the visibly shaken Raja to calm down.

After five minutes, Digvijay said, "Do continue."

"It is like this, sir. We, from the police force, aren't able to do anything about the *Yuvaraja's* atrocities. That's why I came to meet you, hoping you would be able to control him in some way. Could you please help us here?"

It was with sheer will power inherent in most of the royal nobles, that the Raja managed not to squirm. He felt so ashamed to look at the Assistant Commissioner of Police in the eye. It looked like Harischandra couldn't stoop any lower than he already had. His lips drooping in sadness, the Raja said, "I will, Selva Durai. And if I'm unable to make him toe the line, I'll definitely give you a call and you are welcome to return with an arrest warrant and take my son into custody."

Selva Durai got up from his seat, bringing his hands together once again, this time in gratitude. "Thank you so much, Raja Gajanan. You'll be doing the people of Indore a great favour."

My own people! The Gajanan family had ruled over the land for the last four centuries. And each generation of rulers had worked tirelessly which enabled the region and the people to prosper. Harischandra was the first one who was doing exactly the opposite. The Raja felt heartbroken. But no! He sat up straight. He had a responsibility to the society and he couldn't keep quiet any more.

Digvijay sent for his son once the ACP left the palace…

"I have something important to tell you and you'd better take me seriously, son." The Raja spoke to Harischandra in a stern voice. "You…"

Harischandra pushed back his chair noisily, standing up, his rage and fury reflected in his posture. Placing his palms on the desk, he bent his face to the level of his father's and shouted at him, "Why did I even imagine you might have something nice to tell me? I DO NOT WANT TO LISTEN TO ONE MORE OF YOUR BORING LECTURES, DO YOU HEAR ME?"

"Shut up and sit down, Harry," said Digvijay in a firm voice, not too bothered with his son's tantrum. "And listen to what I have to say. Or you will regret it for the rest of your miserable life, I promise."

Harischandra frowned heavily even as his mind worked furiously. Usually, whenever he raised his voice at this father, the older man clammed up. What must have happened today that he was behaving so differently? Finally becoming aware that he didn't really have a choice, Harischandra turned around to pull the chair forward and sat down, waiting for his father to speak.

"ACP Selva Durai was here." The Raja quickly repeated his conversation with the policeman and said, "Didn't you know the girl was bleeding when you left her?"

"Does it really matter now, Father? She's alive and kicking right now, isn't she? Why the hell are you bothered? She's after all, a whore," Harischandra sneered, a mean expression in his steely narrow eyes.

Digvijay shook his head at his son. "I see that your attitude is beyond repair. I called you to tell you something clearly. The next time I receive a complaint against you, I'll disinherit you and throw you out on the streets. Am I clear?" The Raja's words were impactful even though he didn't raise his voice.

Harischandra was stunned to hear what his father had to say, his mind refusing to function for a few minutes. He couldn't believe that the old man would actually do that to him. He stared at the Raja for a long while until his devious mind started ticking again. Looking into his father's steely gaze, Harischandra realised that the other man meant business. What the fuck! He felt a strong urge to kill his father. Maybe he would just do that.

"You wouldn't do that to your only son, would you, Father?" he said, a wily look in his eyes.

"Try me! And you'll know better when you are out begging on the streets," snarled Digvijay, his anger mounting. Not one word of apology had escaped his son lips! It looked like Harischandra would never feel remorse for his evil deeds.

Harischandra didn't respond to his father's taunt, the wheels turning in his head. It looked like it would be best if he toed the line with his parent for at least a while. Not having earned a rupee in his life, the *Yuvaraja* would be truly lost without his inheritance.

Realising it was best to keep his father happy right now at least, Harischandra said, "Okay, Father. I promise to behave."

Phew! Digvijay Gajanan sighed, his shoulders relaxing as the tension drained out from him. For a moment there, he had been worried that he might have to have his own son arrested.

The Raja was not to know that Harischandra was planning to follow the eleventh commandment: not to get caught.

26

Singapore, 2012

"What do you think of the presentation, Rituraj? You think they received it well?" Sitara sat back with a satisfied sigh on the living room sofa of their twin-bedroom suite at the Grand Hyatt. She was totally beat, the whole of her body aching, what with their travelling through last night and the meeting with some prospective sponsors from this morning till late evening. Even before leaving India, she had been working hard over two weeks without taking a break.

Sitara planned to set up a shelter for orphaned girls in Mandvi along with a school for them in the same compound. While she had fifty per cent of the funds ready, she needed some sponsors for the balance amount. A bank with its head office in Singapore had showed an interest in the project and that's why Sitara and Rituraj were here in the garden city.

While Rituraj had managed to garner the interest of the bankers, it was Sitara who had put together a PowerPoint presentation for the CEO and his team. They had promised to give her an answer in two days.

"The presentation was fantastic, Sitara. You did a damn good job," said Rituraj, giving her a smile as he poured premium whisky into two glasses before adding ice and soda.

That was some praise indeed. Rituraj rarely gushed about anything and his compliments were rare. Colour rose up Sitara's cheeks as she smiled back at him in acknowledgement. Leaning her head against the sofa back, she groaned softly when the muscles in her neck protested.

Rituraj looked up from where he was bending over the table where he was placing their glasses. "Is something wrong?" he asked, concern in his gaze as he ran it over her slender body. She looked good enough to eat, having changed from her silk sari into a pair of white cotton pants and a pastel yellow T-shirt, her hair left loose, her face without makeup.

"I'm just tired. My neck's hurting; my whole body actually." With another sigh, Sitara leaned further, stretching her back, trying to find a comfortable position without much success.

"Here, let me help you."

Before Sitara could grasp the meaning of his words, Rituraj had moved behind her to place his hands on her shoulders, applying gentle pressure.

Sitara gasped, sitting up straight with a jerk, absolutely shocked. Her body played traitor, screaming for his touch while her mind fought a failing war against her rejoicing body. "What are you doing, Rituraj?" She turned her head to glare at him, her eyes going wide as they took in his muscular physique clad in a pair of black chinos and white vee-necked T-shirt. The fuzz covering his lean cheeks made him ooze raw masculinity, making her press a hand to her palpitating heart, her body going taut with desire.

Rituraj lifted his hands, palm upwards, giving a shrug. "I'm trying to help you here, removing the kinks in your neck and shoulders. Why don't you turn around and relax and let me do my job?"

Sitara shook her head in protest. What if she melted into a puddle at his feet? She craved his touch, his lovemaking. It had been seven years, three months and twenty-nine days since they made love. Yes, she had been counting the days, months and years, missing his touch terribly. There were many nights she had cried herself to sleep, craving for his arms around her. She simply could not allow him to touch her now.

"Don't!"

Rituraj scowled, his dark eyebrows meeting above his fiery eyes. "Don't be silly, Sitara. I…"

Sitara shook her head vigorously from side to side, grimacing, shutting her eyes so as to not look at his handsome face. "No, Rituraj."

"Is my touch so revolting, Princess Sitara? Is that why you've distanced yourself from me?" Rituraj knew it wasn't anything like that, but he so wanted to provoke a reaction from her. He was desperate to make love to her now that both of them were far away from home. Surely, Sitara couldn't be worried about her ex-husband's reaction, could she?

"Who's being silly now?" Sitara looked at him, her grey eyes shimmering with unshed tears.

He placed his hands once again on her shoulders and pulled her back to lean against the sofa, stroking his hands downwards, increasing the pressure with every touch.

Sitara moaned, revelling in his touch, the pain receding from her shoulders as he applied pressure to all the right points. Feeling his thumbs at the back of her neck, she leaned into his touch, allowing him better access.

Rituraj kneaded her neck and shoulder muscles rhythmically, his palms and fingers tingling with static. He bent down to whisper into her ear, "Have you gone to sleep on me?"

Sitara opened slumberous eyes to look up at him, finding his face too close for comfort. "Ritu, I…"

It was Rituraj who melted when he heard that oft' familiar name which only she used, bending down further to press his mouth to her luscious lips, demanding an entry. He got what he wanted when Sitara lifted her arms to place them around his neck before welcoming him into her mouth.

He gathered her up into his arms and sat down on the sofa before pulling her down on his lap, crushing her pliant body to his hard one without breaking the kiss.

Time stood still as they made love on the sofa, rediscovering each other's body, clothes landing all over the room as they removed their garments in a hurry before Sitara lay on her back on the sofa, Rituraj's body covering hers.

"I've missed you, sweetheart." Rituraj groaned as he buried his face in the valley between her breasts, his hands running down her body from shoulder to thigh.

Sitara swallowed hard, before leaning forward to take a bite of his shoulder, whispering, "Not as much as I've missed you, Ritu."

Rituraj lifted his head to look down at her with pained eyes. "Then why? Why did you push me away? I..."

Sitara pressed a hand over his mouth, shaking her head. "We can't belong together, Ritu. I..."

"Says who?"

Didn't he know Sitara was unfit to be any decent man's wife? And that's what she wanted to be. Rituraj didn't deserve someone as degraded as Sitara in his life.

And, being his lover wasn't an option, all because of her jealous ex-husband. She didn't want Rituraj to get assaulted or even murdered. The truth was that Rituraj definitely deserved someone better than herself. An innocent woman who would make him happy; of whom he would feel proud.

"Answer me, Sitara." Rituraj bent down to take a sharp bite of her sensuous lower lip, making her moan with desire.

Not ready to reply to his question, Sitara ran a tongue over his lips before kissing him passionately.

Rituraj forgot his name, let alone his question as they made torrid love, unable to keep their hands off each other. His mouth at her breasts and his fingers between her legs, Rituraj drove Sitara towards tipping point before withdrawing his hand and plunging his manhood deeply into her vagina, giving a grunt before settling in. "You okay?"

"Ne'er been better," said Sitara, her eyes glowing as she grinned madly at him, curling her legs around his lean waist and crossing her ankles at his back.

His hands on her hips, Rituraj pulled himself out to thrust again, beginning the ritual as old as time as pressure built up within both of them. It wasn't long before they came together, moaning loudly before Rituraj fell against her, totally spent.

"That was simply awesome, Ritu."

He moved to the side and turned his head to face her, his eyebrow raised. "Was it, really?" he asked, half sarcastic.

"Are you saying you didn't like it?" Sitara looked into his eyes searchingly, refusing to believe her own words.

"If both of us like it so much, then why the hell aren't we doing it more often?" He was visibly angry now, his body vibrating against hers, sending a thrill up her spine.

Sitara didn't care for the direction the conversation was taking. She moved away from him to get up. She picked up her pieces of clothing lying around the room and left his on another sofa. She was keen to get dressed so she hurriedly began to pull on her bra and panties.

"Sitara, I asked you a question." Rituraj got up to walk towards her, appearing glorious in his nakedness.

Sitara shut her eyes so that she didn't have to look at him. But his figure was branded behind her eyelids, making her want to wrap her arms around him once again.

Rituraj took her hands in his, effectively stopping her from hooking her bra. With his thumb and forefinger, he pulled the bra off her and threw it over his shoulder, his hands cupping her breasts. "Answer me," he ordered.

Sitara held back, her arms hanging at her sides. But her body seemed to have a mind of its own as it pressed closer into his hands, revelling in his touch even while his rough hands played havoc with her breasts. She bit her upper lip to stop the moan from gushing out of her throat, her hands tightening into fists as she fought with the desire to gather him in her arms.

"You know the answer to your question," she said, finally, realising that he wasn't going to let go of her unless she replied.

Only it didn't work that way as Rituraj bent down to run a damp tongue in a circle over an aureole, round and round, making her desperate for his mouth to close over the tip.

"Ritu…" she groaned, one arm around his neck while the other hand caressed his head, running her fingers through the rough silk of his hair. "Please, Ritu."

He was too angry to oblige her, driving her crazy as he took small bites all around the curve of her breasts, kissing it better as he moved on from one side to the other.

"Rituraj Srivastava!" Sitara grabbed a fistful of his hair and pulled his head up.

"What? You don't like my kisses?" he asked, a mischievous smile on his face. He took his hands off and moved a couple of inches away from her to say, "Let me not bother you, in that case." His hot gaze was on the turgid tips of her breasts which responded with alacrity, turning painfully tight, making Sitara moan with longing.

"Ritu! I'm going to kill you if you don't make love to me, right now." Sitara fell against his chest, her hands on his shoulders as she nibbled at a flat nipple.

His hands in her hair as he pulled her closer to his body, Rituraj asked, "Is that what you want? Why didn't you tell me so?" a trace of laughter in his voice.

Sitara couldn't help the answering laughter in her voice as she said, "I might just murder you one of these days," before burying her face in his shoulder. He was too damn irresistible. She wondered how she had managed to keep him at arms' length for so many years.

But the smile vanished from her face after they made love once again, this time in Sitara's bedroom. It was all okay, here in Singapore, far away from Harischandra. But it couldn't happen in Baroda, not with her ex-husband getting to know every single detail of her life. She could not place Rituraj's life at risk, not again.

Sitara didn't know that Rituraj had already taken the necessary precautions, because he hadn't mentioned anything to her about it.

27

Indore, 2010

Harischandra was seated at a popular dance bar when Rituraj stepped in, and walked directly up to him. The *Yuvaraja* was absolutely drunk, having been sitting at the bar since seven in the evening when it opened its doors to the public. He was having the time of his life, watching the bar dancer, Akila, doing the pole dance. The other customers were familiar with the Gajanan prince and his tantrums. Hence, they not only kept their distance from him, but also from Akila, turning their attention to the other three dancers.

Rituraj went and sat on the barstool to the left of Harischandra's. "Good evening, Gajanan."

"Who the hell are you?" Harischandra turned bleary eyes to glare at Rituraj in the dim light before recognition hit him. "You! Get out, you motherfucker. How dare you talk to me? I'm royalty and you're nothing but..." Harishchandra's pent-up venom flowed out in full force.

Rituraj's lip curled in disgust even as he raised a supercilious brow at the other man. "Listen, I have some important information you need," he said, getting directly to the point.

Harischandra threw back his head and laughed uproariously. "I don't need a damn thing from you, you son of a bitch. I'll have you beaten to a pulp if you don't leave the bar right now. I…"

"Just shut up and listen," said Rituraj, removing a large envelope from his backpack. Pulling out half a dozen photographs from it, he threw them on the bar in front of Harischandra. "Have a look at these before you utter one more word. I don't think you'd want me to share these with your father, Raja Gajanan, would you?"

It wasn't easy, holding back his temper to check out the photographs. While Harischandra wanted to plant his fist in Rituraj's face, he was smart enough to know that the other man would never take it lying down and he simply wasn't a match for the trained boxer. Clenching his jaw, he turned to check the pictures. Unable to believe his eyes, the *Yuvaraja* quickly picked up the colourful print. It was of Rabri and him on the terrace, his cock pushed deep into her throat. There was no way that anyone could mistake the people in the picture. He quickly ran through the five other pictures to see himself in a compromising position with different women; one where he had a whip in his hand while the woman was on her knees, her hands together as if she was begging for mercy. Which she actually had been at that instant!

WHAT THE FUCK!

The high he had been on after many drinks seemed to have disappeared that very minute, dragging him back to earth forcefully.

He turned his head to Rituraj, his eyes red with fury. "I'll have you killed for this, you dickhead. I…"

Rituraj laughed softly, shaking his head. "I don't think so, Gajanan. I have more of those and also the originals saved."

"What the fuck do you want?" Harischandra snarled at his ex-wife's bodyguard, his eyes promising murder.

"Your promise that you won't come anywhere near Princess Sitara Devi or me." Not that Rituraj believed Harischandra was capable of keeping a promise. But he was certain the *Yuvaraja* wouldn't be keen to be disinherited.

Harischandra lifted his middle finger, shouting by now. "I knew it. I always knew you were after that cunt. I…"

Rituraj lifted a hand and slapped him hard. "That's for besmirching the Gaekwad Princess's name. I think I'll visit your father. Now, if you will excuse me." He got off the stool to pick up the photos and shoved them back into the envelope.

"Wait a minute." Harischandra called out in desperation, holding his burning left cheek. "Stay away from my father, do you hear?"

Rituraj turned around with a raised eyebrow. "Do I have your promise?"

Harischandra gave him a small nod, hatred in his eyes.

"I didn't hear you," said Rituraj, his eyes cool at he stared the *Yuvaraja* down.

"I promise," said Harischandra in a pathetic whisper, fully aware about not having a choice.

"*Yuvaraja* Harischandra Gajanan, remember one thing. If in this life time you even think about Princess Sitara Devi or me you will only end up shortening your own life. Goodbye!"

Rituraj left, never looking back. He would have been surprised if he had been privy to Harischandra's thoughts at that very moment. The Gajanan prince decided then and there he wouldn't have anything to do with his ex-wife or her Man Friday. Neither of them was worth the trouble.

28

Rituraj and Sitara were celebrating their success. The bankers had agreed not only to sponsor fifty per cent of the costs of setting up the shelter and school, but had also committed to pay the total yearly maintenance for the next five years.

"Cheers," said Sitara, lifting her glass of sparkling wine to Rituraj.

"Cheers, Princess," he responded, touching the tip of his glass to hers as he looked deeply into her eyes.

Despite the hot colour running up her cheeks, Sitara's gaze turned sultry as she returned his look with equal fervour.

"Did I tell you how gorgeous you look?" he said throatily, his eyes taking in her silk attire in brilliant red. It made her skin glow.

"You mean I look better than you do?" she asked, grinning mischievously at him. He wore a three-piece suit in dark grey, a pristine white shirt and a maroon tie with grey motifs. His hair was brushed back neatly while his black-framed glasses only added to his dashing looks.

Rituraj grinned back at her, lifting his glass once again in a toast before drinking from it. He had dragged her all around Singapore during the past three days, not letting her do any work. They went to Sentosa Island by cable car and spent a whole day there. They also visited Jurong Bird Park and the Singapore Botanical Garden. They travelled on local buses and metro, which was in itself a novelty for both of them.

They had made torrid love late into the nights, Rituraj refusing to listen to any of Sitara's protests. In the end, she gave in only because she couldn't resist him.

They finished their dinner quickly before going up to their suite on the twentieth floor. "Would you like to go for a walk?" asked Rituraj.

Sitara stepped forward and into his arms, her own going around his neck. She lifted her face up to his, saying, "Maybe later. I want you now."

"You do know I'm all yours, don't you?" he asked, his voice hoarse with longing as he pressed his forehead to hers.

Sitara sighed, burying her face in his shoulder. Couldn't they simply hide here in Singapore? Why go back to India, after all?

"I want to marry you, sweetheart." Rituraj whispered in her ear, running his hand through her silky hair. "Will you be my wife?"

Sitara jumped back in protest. No! This is what she craved and it also worried the daylights out of her.

"No!" she croaked, her throat choking up with emotion, before clearing her throat and repeating loudly, "NO!"

Rituraj frowned heavily, his dark eyebrows bunching up together in a straight line. "Why not? Is it because you don't love me?" he asked, heavy sarcasm in his voice.

"Don't be an idiot, Ritu. That's not true."

"Then?" He moved closer, trying to take her back in his arms, but she wouldn't let him.

Sitara took a few more steps backwards and said, "I told you before. And I'm telling you again: we both don't belong with each other."

"And why is that? Because you are royalty and I'm not?"

Sitara began shaking her head even before he finished his sentence. "That's utter crap and you very well know that."

"Then why won't you marry me?"

"Harry…"

"You can stop worrying about your ex-husband. You have me by your side, don't you? Don't worry about that creep!"

Sitara's mouth fell open in surprise. "Are you sure?"

Rituraj smiled. "I'm your bodyguard. It's the least I can do for you."

Sitara gave him an adoring look. "You know you are way more than that. You are my Man Friday."

"Okay, is that a good enough qualification to be your husband, Princess Sitara Devi?" he asked, tongue-in-cheek.

Sitara turned the other way. How to make him understand? He didn't deserve someone like her. She turned once again to face him. "Listen, Ritu. I'm unfit to be any decent man's wife. Why don't you get married to someone better than me? Someone…"

"Shuddup, Princess. Why the hell would I marry someone else when it's only you I want?" Rituraj raised his voice to shout at her.

Sitara gave a shake of her head, as she suddenly understood Rituraj was angry with her. She walked up to him and placed a pacifying hand on his shoulder. "Forget about marriage for now. Love me, please?" She lifted her face up for his kiss.

Rituraj sighed, his anger draining out of his system as desire took over. Pulling her into his arms, he kissed her hard, deciding to shelve the subject of marriage for the time being.

Baroda, 2018

Sitara paced up and down the terrace, feeling completely restless. She had gone to bed at eleven but hadn't been able to sleep. There was a strange excitement bubbling from deep within her while she felt so much lighter than before. The main reason was the incredible news that Harischandra—the demon who had haunted her life all this long, despite their divorce—was no more.

There was nothing to stop her from being in a relationship with Rituraj. As for the rest of the world, she didn't give a damn. It was Rituraj she loved and it was Rituraj she wanted. And as for him… Sitara smiled to herself. He wanted to marry her. And had asked her not once, but very many times.

She grimaced. He hadn't liked it at all when she refused him, each time, every time. But then, Sitara knew for a fact that she wasn't wifely material, especially for someone as pure and untarnished as Rituraj.

But!

Sitara stopped pacing, coming to a quick decision. Walking into her bedroom, she wrapped a matching silken dressing gown around her sleeveless nightdress before stepping out. Racing down the staircase, she opened the main door and let herself out silently.

The outhouse Rituraj lived in was only a couple of hundred metres away from the palace. Thrilled to see a light burning on the first floor, Sitara rang the bell, clutching a hand over her furiously beating heart. As she waited for the door to open, she couldn't help recalling their trip to Singapore, the last time they made love. Six more years gone after that, she thought to herself, her lips drooping.

But then, how could she agree to sleep in his arms, right here under the nose of Harischandra's spy?

She had got to know about Shantaram after Rituraj moved out of the palace. "Is that why you offered to shift to the outhouse?" Sitara had asked Rituraj.

"Hmm… yes."

"How did you guess that Harry had sent the servant?"

Rituraj quickly explained how he had caught Shantaram eavesdropping outside the library window. "I became sure when he said he's from Baroli which is not all that far away from Indore. Later, I spoke to Brijmohan and Nirupama. Nirupama confirmed that a distant relative of hers begged her to take the boy to work here in the palace. They hadn't spoken about wages and all that because I was in hospital and you were too busy."

"Why haven't you thrown him out yet, Rituraj?" Sitara had asked, thoroughly angry and frustrated. Couldn't she escape her husband, ever?

"That was my first instinct. Then I sat down to think. Right now, we know Shantaram is Gajanan's spy. If we chuck him out, chances are high that Harischandra might send someone else or even strike at us from a different angle. Doesn't it make sense to keep the man and pretend not to know anything?"

Sitara smiled, her gaze full of admiration. "How come you weren't born in a royal family? You are so good at strategizing."

He laughed. "You can call me a warrior, most suited for the role of a bodyguard. What say?"

She nodded, smiling wider. "Oh yes! That you are."

"So, let's keep him and feed Shantaram with all the information we want Harischandra to consume."

"And that's why you shifted into the outhouse."

He gave a nod. "That's right."

Sitara pulled herself back to the present when she heard him pull open the heavy metal bolt on the front door. She felt a thrill of shiver run down her spine when she saw Rituraj standing on the other side wearing only a pair of shorts, exposing his broad and hairy chest and long, muscular legs to her eager gaze.

"Hello!" The word came out in a croak as Sitara's throat dried up as she felt a zing of excitement.

"Hey! Come on in." Rituraj opened the door wider to let his late-night visitor in. It was almost one.

Sitara walked into the hall, her eyes running all around, refusing to look at him.

Rituraj stood there, his hands on his hips as he ran his hungry eyes over her slender figure. "What's up, sweetheart? Unable to sleep?"

"Ritu!" She flung herself into his arms the moment she heard him say, 'sweetheart'.

He gathered her close to his body, pressing his lips to the top of her silky head. "What happened?"

Sudden laughter gurgled up her throat to burst forth. She lifted her face off his chest to look into his eyes. "Harry's death happened. I feel so free!"

"You have been free all these years."

She shook her head. "No, Ritu. I haven't been free at all. There was always this fear of when he would strike. The way one fears a cobra. I feel like dancing with joy."

He grinned, looking at her animated face. "I never knew you were a bloodthirsty warrior princess."

Sitara laughed some more. "Is that how I come across?"

"Absolutely!"

"Have you ever made love to a warrior princess before?" she asked, pouting her lips invitingly as she gave him a sultry look from the corner of her eyes.

"Let me see," said Rituraj, his gaze turning mischievous. "I've made love to an experienced princess who stole my virginity. And then to this social entrepreneur who was drunk on her success. And after that…" he shook his head, his lips drooping, "Zilch!"

"Aww! You poor baby! Why is that? Couldn't you find anyone else to love you?" She pressed her lips to his cheek and traced a tongue down his rough jawline before stopping at his chin.

"The woman I want, have always wanted, has made it clear she doesn't want me." He let go of Sitara to take a few steps back.

"You know that's so not true." Her arms felt empty now that he had stepped away from her.

"Isn't it? You never sought my arms after we returned from Singapore." There was intense pain his voice. And he had gone to her, just once, only to be rejected. She had refused to let Rituraj touch her after they returned from the trip.

"You very well know why Ritu. Harry was keeping a watch over us. I would have killed myself if he had hurt you one more time."

Rituraj turned back swiftly and placed his hands on her shoulders, then shook her hard. "Are you saying you were scared of that slimy fox hurting me?" he growled, a deep frown on his face. "He wouldn't have dared to."

"He did break your bones. Or have you forgotten?" Sitara was shouting by now.

Rituraj shook his head at her. "But you don't understand. I took care of him. I made sure he'd never come after us."

She squinted up at him, a heavy frown on her face. "What did you do? And why don't I know anything about it?"

Rituraj let go of her, then turned away and paced the hall restlessly. Had he made a mistake in not telling Sitara about meeting Harischandra and threatening to expose him to his father? What a stupid thing to have done! If he had told her, would Sitara have become his? Had he wasted all these years only because of his silence and stupidity? His only excuse was that he hadn't wanted to draw Sitara's attention towards the ex-husband whom she hated and feared. After all, it was his duty to protect her as her bodyguard. He didn't have to give her all the details.

An expression of remorse on his face, Rituraj walked up to her and said, "I think you'd better sit down." Going to the bar in the corner, he poured a snifter of brandy and brought it back to her. "Drink up! You might need it."

"Why? What happened?" she asked, taking the glass from him and sipping from it.

"Finish it."

She took his advice and did just that before giving the empty glass back to him. "Will you tell me before I die of curiosity?" she asked, her eyes never leaving his tense face.

"As long as you don't murder me." He quickly told her all about meeting Harischandra in Indore and showing him the compromising pictures. He explained how he had literally blackmailed the Gajanan prince, threatening to show the pictures to his father if he didn't get off their backs. "And he agreed though it killed him."

"He did? And you believed him?"

Rituraj shrugged. "And why not? Anyway, he never did trouble us after that, did he?"

"Probably because he was too busy doing other things," she said bitterly. "Do you know his father's dead?"

Rituraj gave a small nod, frowning. What was she getting at? "So? Are you saying that he could have harmed us after that? Why would he want to hold on to his anger for so long?"

Sitara shook her head. "You don't know Harry like I used to. He's the devil incarnate. Do you know how his father died?"

"I don't know and frankly, I don't care." Rituraj glared at her.

"Harry killed him, Ritu. He poisoned his own father."

"What the hell?!" That shook him, badly. "How do you know?"

"Prince Rajvardhan Thakore told me. An old servant from the Gajanan Palace, Hansraj, also gave his testimony to the magistrate."

"Oh my God!" If Harischandra was capable of murdering his own father, it meant that he was capable of turning towards Sitara and him too. What a vengeful bastard! No wonder Sitara rejoiced in his death.

He walked up to her and pulled her into his arms. "I didn't know, sweetheart. No wonder you were worried. And to think you lived with that evil excuse of a man for two years! It must have been pure torture." He hugged her tightly.

She buried her face in his shoulder, her arms around his waist. "Please make love to me, Ritu."

He lifted his head to look down at her. "On one condition."

The expression in her eyes turned wary as she stared into his eyes, almost sure of what was coming. "What?"

"I want to marry you."

"Please Ritu. I told you that's not possible."

"Why? Are you saying that I'm fit to be your lover, but not your husband?" He refused to let go when she tried to get out of his arms.

"It's me, Ritu," she said in a pathetic whisper, tears shimmering in her eyes. "I'm the one who's fit to be your lover but not your wife."

"Sitara! Sweetheart! Are you mad? Why do you say that?"

"Did you not say just now that I was married to an evil excuse of a man? That's so true, Ritu," she said, her voice shaking with unshed tears, "He dragged me so deep into the depths of debauchery far beyond your pristine imagination." The tears poured down freely, Sitara unable to stop them. "You wouldn't want to know. I…"

"Can't you leave the past behind? It's been eighteen years since you returned home. And Dr. King did believe you had successfully overcome the scars." He paused to give her a keen glance, "Do you still get nightmares?"

Sitara smiled through her tears, shaking her head. "No, I don't. Something for which I'm grateful to you and Dr. King!"

"Then why don't you let him go? He's dead after all."

She frowned up at him, not able to grasp his meaning. "Where am I holding on to him? I want to dance and sing that he's dead, gone forever."

"But you refuse to make a life for yourself, get yourself a life partner. Why is that?" Rituraj was logic personified.

"Er… um… Ritu, you don't understand. I…"

"Then why don't you make me understand?" he asked, "I'm all ears."

She tried to pull out of his arms only he wouldn't let her go. She told him in a furious whisper the atrocities she had suffered at Harischandra's hands; how Rabri had been part of the threesome in bed on most nights. "I hated my body those times, Ritu. I…"

Unable to help himself, Rituraj bent down to kiss her passionately, his arms like iron bands around her.

When they came up for air, she continued, "It all felt so dirty, Ritu. Until you… till that night we made love for the first time, I thought myself incapable of liking sex, let alone enjoying it. Your passion helped me find my soul, Ritu. You have given me so much and," she lifted her face to kiss him on his mouth, "I thank you for it. I'll be happy to be your lover, till you find yourself a good girl for a wife."

Rituraj burst out laughing, much to her chagrin.

"What's so funny?" she frowned at him.

"It looks like I don't want a good girl for a wife. I want this bad girl who's been married before, the one who deflowered me." More laughter rumbled forth from within him. "I've never slept with another woman in my life. Will you make an honest man of me, Princess Sitara Devi?"

"I think you are stark, raving mad. Didn't you hear anything that I said just now? About my life in Indore. My…"

He pressed a hand over her mouth, effectively stopping her from talking further. "Are you really so fascinated with your life as Gajanan's wife that you need to compulsively talk about it?" he asked, grinning down at her.

"Don't you understand that I've led an absolutely sinful life unlike a decent woman? Why don't you take me seriously?" Sitara glared up at his laughing countenance.

"Hmm. Let me see. Was it your doing? Did you choose to lead such a life?"

"Of course not, you idiot. You know very well it was forced on me. And Rabri too. I..."

"Exactly! And I rest my case."

Sitara stared at him. Had she heard him right? It wasn't long before her frown cleared and a small smile appeared on her face. "Are you saying what I think you are saying?" she asked in an incredulous voice. Was there a way to be absolved of everything? Become completely free of Harischandra and his hold on her life?

Rituraj gave her a gentle smile. "How can you hold yourself responsible for their actions? Come on, sweetheart, you are way too smart for that."

"Aren't I?!" Sitara jumped up to throw her arms around his neck. "Yes, oh yes! I want to be your wife. But..."

He bit her lower lip, growling, "What now? Can't a man find some peace and happiness without conditions?"

Sitara laughed, kissing him back passionately. "Can we live together in secret for some time? It will be so exciting." Her dark grey eyes danced with mischief, her heart beating like a drum.

"Whatever you want, as long as you agree to marry me." He lifted her in his arms to carry her up the stairs to his bedroom.

"Whatever? Are you sure? What if I... mfft..."

Rituraj didn't give her a chance to speak again for the next couple of hours.

EPILOGUE

Baroda, 2019

Harshvardhan danced the most at his sister's and best friend's wedding, his wife Dayanita partnering him throughout.

He hugged Rituraj. "I'm so glad *di* agreed to marry you, finally."

"As if she really had a choice," said Rituraj cheekily, throwing an arm around her shoulders to pull Sitara close to his side. They had got married at the Gaekwad Palace an hour back, by the Arya Samaj rites, with about fifty-odd guests attending the ceremony.

Lawyer Vishal Trivedi stepped forward to congratulate the newly married couple. "Congratulations Princess Sitara Devi and Rituraj. I'm so happy for you both. There's a private matter I need to discuss with all of you," he said, including the four of them in the conversation.

"Can it wait until the wedding lunch is over?" asked Sitara, a wide smile on her face. She glowed in a cream coloured Banarasi silk sari with a red and gold border, and a splendid set of diamonds and rubies gracing her throat, ears and wrists.

"Sure," said Vishal, smiling at the happy bride.

It was almost three in the afternoon when the lawyer sat down to talk to Sitara, Rituraj, Harshvardhan and Dayanita. "I've had this legal paper with me from 2004. Raja Manvendra Singh had asked me to draft it and then signed it in my presence."

Harshvardhan turned his curious gaze on the lawyer. "Why didn't you give it to us before now?"

"There's a reason for it. The Raja had a condition. I was supposed to hand over this paper only if and when Princess Sitara Devi married Rituraj Srivastava."

Both the Prince and Princess of Gaekwad were absolutely stunned on hearing this.

"*Bapuji* thought I might get married to Rituraj?" Sitara asked the lawyer, wonder in her voice.

"*Rajaji* wanted it, actually." It was Rituraj who answered her in a quiet voice. "As did Rani *ma*."

Harshvardhan grinned, not really surprised to hear that while Sitara gave her new husband a startled glance. "What? When?"

Rituraj took her hand in his. "A few weeks before they left on that fatal trip. They were planning to speak with you as soon as they came back."

"Then why didn't you?" Sitara asked him, surprise on her face.

"I didn't think you'd have believed me." It was with difficulty that he kept the tremor out of his voice.

Sitara tightened her hold on his hand, pressing her thumb over the back pacifyingly, silent apology in her eyes.

Vishal Trivedi removed an envelope from his briefcase and handed it over to Harshvardhan. "Can you please read it loudly, Prince Harshvardhan?"

Harshvardhan pulled the single sheet of paper from the envelope and opened it, a soft smile on his face when he saw his father's signature right at the bottom.

He read from it:

Annexure to my last will and testament. I have left instructions with the Gaekwad family lawyer to have this document opened only in the event of my daughter, Princess Sitara Devi Gaekwad, marrying Rituraj Srivastava.

In case this happy event takes place, I will the Baroda palace and outhouse to Sitara and Rituraj Srivastava, along with all the furniture; with the consent of my son, Prince Harshvardhan Singh Gaekwad.

"Of course, you have my consent," said Harshvardhan, pumping his fist in the air, handing the paper back to the lawyer after seeing there wasn't much else in it except some legal mumbo jumbo. He got up to hug his sister. "You have the right to live here, *di*. And I'm so glad that *Bapuji* understood that." He turned to Rituraj and bumped a fist against his, giving him a wide grin.

Neither Rituraj nor Sitara were surprised at Harshvardhan's large heart. But then, wasn't he the son of the Raja and Rani who had fostered their accountant's child and made him what he was today?

"So, queen of my heart! Are you happy?" asked Rituraj, kissing his wife on her forehead as she lay on his chest that night, her eyes only half-open as she looked at him, a satiated smile on her face.

"Absolutely! I love you, Ritu. And thank you so much for your patience and persistence. I…"

Rituraj groaned in protest. "Need you begin the thank you speech immediately after telling me the words I've been waiting to hear all my life?"

"What?" Sitara sat up to ask him, a confused expression on her face. "I don't understand. If it hadn't been for your persistence, I wouldn't have become your wife today. What are you cribbing about?"

He gave an exaggerated sigh, reaching out to cup her breast before moving forward to draw his tongue over the tip. "Go back a little. What did you tell me before you began your thank you speech?"

Sitara frowned, thinking for a few seconds before the light dawned on her face. With a mischievous smile, she said, "Oh that! Okay, I understand what you mean."

"What did you understand?" he grumbled, nipping her shoulder.

"You heard me the first time."

He lifted his head to look at her. "And what if I want to hear it again?"

"You just have to ask, you idiot. I love you, Ritu." She hugged him, pressing her body close to his and her lips to his mouth. "I love you more than anything in the world, my darling Ritu."

"And I love you, my sweetheart," swore her Man Friday, "I promise to cherish you all my life."

THE END

OTHER BOOKS
BY
SUNDARI
VENKATRAMAN

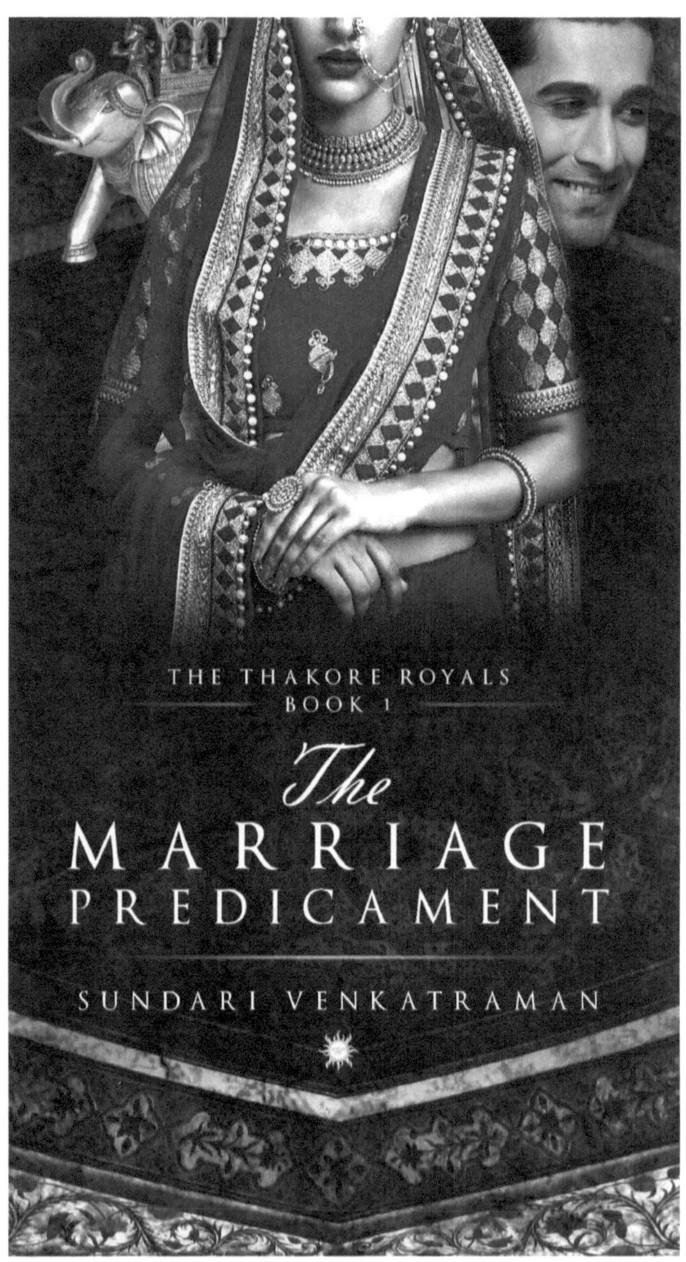
THE THAKORE ROYALS
BOOK 1
The
MARRIAGE
PREDICAMENT
SUNDARI VENKATRAMAN

Princess Yashodhara Jadeja of Bhatewar isn't at all keen to get married. With her tarnished past, she knows that her married life would never be easy. But, between her father's Will and her mother's persuasion, she's left with no choice.

Prince Indrajeet Thakore of Udaipur agrees to meet Yashodhara as a prospective wife after his grandmother, Rajmata Santhini Devi, persuades him. While no cymbals crash at their first meeting, the couple grow to like and respect one another before they agree to tie the knot.

Both belong to royal families and both have responsibilities. Over and above all that, their marriage is plagued by a predicament, just as Yashodhara had expected. It looks like they can lead a happy married life only if the princess is willing to break a promise. Will she be able to do that? And will Prince Indrajeet continue to love her once he gets to know about her past?

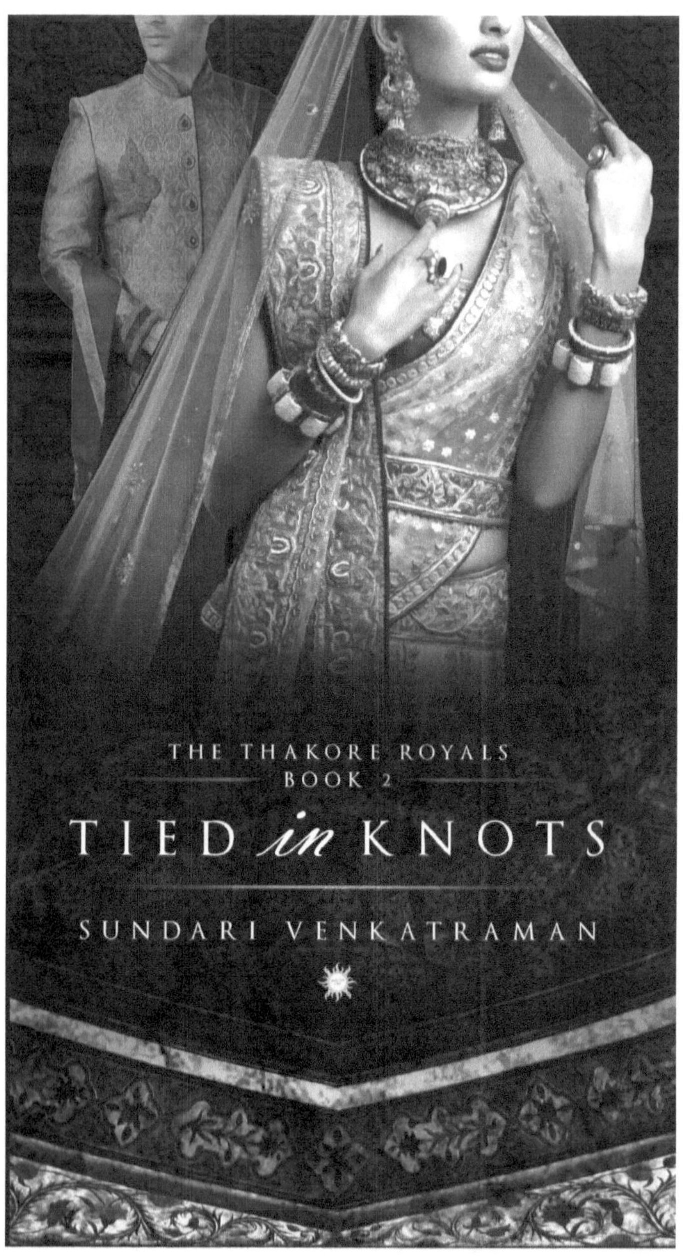

THE THAKORE ROYALS
BOOK 2
TIED *in* KNOTS
SUNDARI VENKATRAMAN

When Princess Chitrangada Vasudeva of Jodhana runs away from her bodyguards in the European city of Zurich, the last thing she expects is to be incarcerated with a stranger in his hotel suite for three days and nights.

Prince Rajvardhan Thakore of Udaipur is on his way to take part in the ice polo event at St. Moritz and plans to take a much-needed break in Zurich. He's thrown for a toss when he stops his car to help a damsel in distress. A few minutes into the encounter, he finds out that "Princess" is anything but a helpless female.

Sparks fly, and how!

Until that morning when Princess simply ups and leaves Rajvardhan without a contact number or a forwarding address. He doesn't even know her real name.

And then they meet again under the most unusual of circumstances back in Rajasthan, during Chitrangada's engagement to Raja Harischandra Gajanan of Indore. Even stranger is the fact that her fiancé is more her father's contemporary than hers.

Will the Thakore prince's endeavor to make the Vasudeva princess his own succeed under the circumstances?

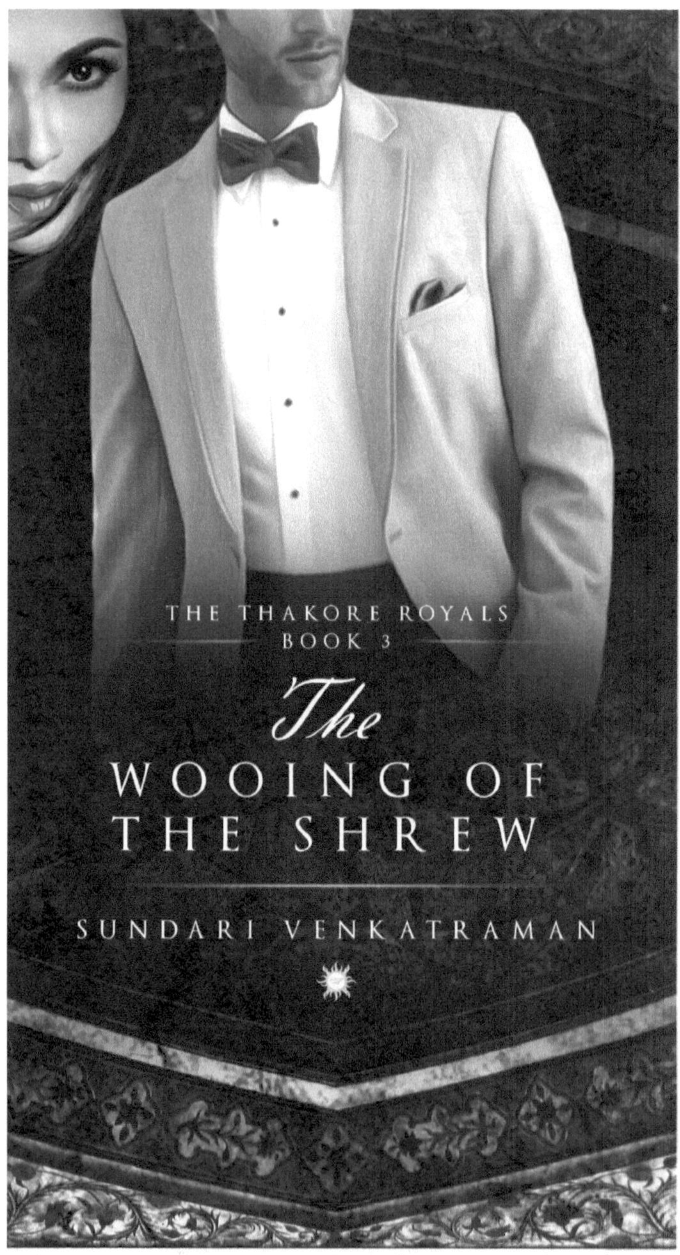

THE THAKORE ROYALS
BOOK 3
The
WOOING OF
THE SHREW
SUNDARI VENKATRAMAN

ayanita Thakore is a prickly princess who doesn't care for the idea of any man getting close to her... until Prince Harshvardhan Singh Gaekwad turns up in her life.

Sparks fly even at their first meeting when the Princess of Udaipur clashes with the Prince of Baroda.

He falls in love with the fiery princess while she fights her attraction to him tooth and nail.

He woos her, beguiles her, cherishes her...

...while the princess feels that maybe he couldn't love such a tempestuous woman such as herself.

But before they could cross the great divide and get to know each other, something happens, something terrible that might just blow their lives apart.

Do they have a chance at a happily ever after?

Connect with Sundari Venkatraman here:

Sundari Venkatraman Books

Sundari Venkatraman Books

https://www.sundarivenkatraman.in

Author Sundari Venkatraman

@sundarivenkat

@sundarivenkatraman

sundarivenkat@gmail.com

www.ingramcontent.com/pod-product-compliance
Lightning Source LLC
Chambersburg PA
CBHW051151130726
47988CB00005B/2085